MIND OF MERCUSINE

STARSIDE SAGA #3

ERIC KENT EDSTROM

To J

1

—————

DELICIOUS ONE

The gull flies. The Divide sweeps by and Moonside hides. Beneath foggy shrouds it resides, while Starside shines and thrives, a hive of busy lives.

Alive! cries the gull. Alive!

The day dies and a raven flies high, high, high.

The gull swoops low over Gristenside and cries, Kila Sigh! Arise! Arise!

INSTINCT TOLD Kila that midnight drew near. A life spent thieving in darkness had trained Kila to wakefulness while the sun was down. The adventures of the past few weeks—as exhausting as they'd been—had not changed that. In fact, so much weighed upon her mind she couldn't sleep much during daylight, either.

But that wasn't why she was awake now, lying on

her cot in the novitiates' ward of the Baths of Ori. That wasn't why she was staring into the pure blackness of her room.

It wasn't Ragin's soft snores, either. Having lived in close quarters with her brother, Wen, for her entire life, such sounds were a comfort to her. It wasn't the fact she was back in the hands of the Sensuals of Ori. As much as she hated the idea of being trapped here, at least she was safe from the various threats lurking about in the city.

The Hargothe, for instance.

That name alone made her skin crawl. She pulled her soft blanket to her chin and shifted to get Nax's weight off her chest. The small gray cat stretched and elongated, hind claws digging into Kila's bare thigh. Such pain was a mere annoyance these days. She begrudged the cat nothing. The poor thing had drowned, or nearly so. Only Kila's instinctive use of the mercus—and a tiny bit of *filla*—had spared the cat's life.

The Hargothe. The name returned to her. The Voluptuary of Ori had told Kila a little about the man. Kila had felt his mind upon hers. Twice. She never wanted to experience such a violation again. She was thankful for the queller ring the Voluptuary had loaned her. Though it blocked her from the mercus and the heightened senses it brought, at least the ring protected her from intruding minds.

And yet . . . thoughts of the Hargothe did not keep

her awake. She'd only seen him once in person, thank Til. She knew what he looked like. And she had seen a flash of a vision, sent from Henley to Huff to Nax to her. A withered old man on a bed. More skeleton than flesh. Kila knew if she got close enough she could kill him. Except he was certainly well-guarded. Henley's vision had also shown two strong men in the room, both acolytes in the Way of Til.

Henley's vision had been more than sight. It had encompassed all the senses, including a rending pain unlike anything Kila had felt before.

Henley had come looking for her, and he'd run afoul of the Way of Til. Why? She didn't have the first clue.

But Henley's predicament wasn't what kept her awake.

The fine hairs on her arms kept standing up as waves of gooseflesh tingled across her skin. She had to fight the instinct to cover her head. But there was no threat here.

She couldn't escape the feeling that someone was looking for her. No . . . that someone was *coming* for her.

With the queller on her finger, it couldn't be the mercus telling her this. She sat up. Nax came close to consciousness and sent Kila an incoherent stab of annoyance before going back to sleep.

Dressed in the nightclothes of a novitiate of Ori, Kila felt naked. She longed for shirt and trousers. She pulled the blanket to her chin and held very still. She cocked her head. Listening. She must have heard something to wake her, something that resounded in the realm of instinct. Silence now.

She mistrusted the quiet. It felt false. Relying on such feelings had served her well in the past. She stood from the cot and padded to the door. Nax's irritation passed through her as the cat came fully awake.

Someone is in the hallway, Kila sent to the cat.

Nax slipped from the cot and rubbed against Kila's bare calf, a warm stroke of comfort. *Who?*

Do you smell anything odd?

Aside from the boy?

Nax had not made up her mind about Ragin, so she occasionally made sideways insults about him.

Kila ignored the comment, ears pricked for the slightest footstep. She found herself toying with the queller on her finger. The Voluptuary had warned her never to remove it. This seemed like the perfect time to do so. She needed her mercus senses.

Light, Nax sent.

Kila looked down. Sure enough, the faintest haze of light shone beneath the door. The color of it stopped her from removing the queller. A greenish blue, like the waters of the Brinsto Bay on a sunny morning. It shined at a hard angle, casting minute shadows from the imperfections in the stone tiles of the floor.

The Sensuals used mercus light and whale oil. The first was always white, like the brilliant core of a diamond. The latter burned amber. Kila had never seen this color of light before. Nax recoiled and hissed.

Hush! Kila sent.

The cat silenced herself, but Kila sensed her slink away to hide under Kila's cot. The noise had awoken Ragin, who mumbled unintelligibly.

Kila slipped away from the door and knelt by his cot. Even with the weird green light coming under the door more strongly, she couldn't see him. She put a hand where she hoped his chest was, found his forearm. She followed it to his shoulder, then head. Covering his mouth with her hand, she pressed her lips to his ear. "Something is outside our door."

He tried to jerk his head away, but she held firm. "Keep quiet. Nod if you understand." A pause. A nod. She removed her hand.

The light continued to grow, forming a sharp greenish outline at the base of the door where the gap was widest. But now lines of light were creeping along the hinge side of the door and the top. Whatever was making the light had to be just outside.

Ragin eased down from his cot to crouch next to her. His head bonked into hers and they both let out pained gasps. Suddenly his hands were on her head, twisting her face away. His breath was hot on her ear as he whispered. "Is that mercusine?"

A stupid question. The light *had* to be mercusine. Just because she'd only seen it a brilliant white didn't mean it couldn't be other colors. "Yes. But . . . I saw

Goolsoy make light. It was white, and just a tiny amount made him very tired. I don't think he could do that."

"How about the Voluptuary?"

Maybe. Kila hadn't yet seen the woman do anything with the mercus. She remembered Goolsoy talking about Sensuals working together to combine their power. But none of that explained what was happening in the hallway outside her room.

The light now pierced three sides of the door. The interior of the room was awash with a greenish blue glow. It colored Ragin's face and gleamed from Nax's eyes. The cat darted from the cover of Kila's cot to hide under Ragin's.

The top edge of the door came alight as the door slowly swung open. Kila's hand clamped Ragin's.

Light flooded in, blinding her. She held up a hand to shield her eyes, but it did little good. She could see nothing. A smell wafted in, dark and earthy. But also tinged with the bitter taste of a burnt-out flashtaper.

"Under the cot," Ragin said.

Kila didn't argue. Didn't even think about it. She flattened herself and squeezed under the narrow bed. There was little enough room for one person under it. Ragin squeezed against the wall and pulled her in by the waist. In any other circumstance, she would have elbowed him in the gut. But here, in the face of the weird intrusion of light, she found his warmth comforting.

The light filled the doorway now and the smell of something burning—like hair or meat fallen on a fire—filled the room. She hated being blind. Her hand went to the queller. Ragin's hand closed over hers, keeping her from removing the ring. "Remember what the Voluptuary said."

Now she did elbow him. Not too hard, just enough to make him release her hand. He grunted and coughed. She pinched the ring between forefinger and thumb and started to twist it off. As it slipped over her knuckle, the zing of the mercus slammed into her mind. The smell of burnt hair assaulted her nose. The greenish light took on deeper hues, turning to violet at the center of the doorway.

Sound came to her as if wax plugs had been pulled from her ears.

The sound of breathing, heavy and rumbling, alerted her to the presence of something not at all human just outside the door. And now a footstep. But not any human foot or shoe would make that sound. It had the distinct report of a hoof on stone, as if a horse or steer was in the hallway.

A deep voice full amusement spoke into her mind: *He said you were delicious . . .*

Another clop of hoof. Now closer. The light in the door grew to unbearable intensity. It reflected off the walls with such brightness, Kila was certain the bricks would melt. And yet no heat came from the light. In fact, an iciness had fingered its way into the room.

Clop. Clop.

He said you were powerful.

"What's happening?" Ragin whispered.

Kila found she was holding her breath, fist squeezing around the queller, the other clamped around Ragin's hand which pressed to her abdomen as she pushed back against him, trying to hide deeper under the cot. She sensed that Nax was behind Ragin's knees, curled into a ball.

Clop. Clop.

There you are. The feeling of menacing laughter filled her mind. This was nothing like the presence of Nax, and very different from the greasy touch of the Hargothe. For one, it was loud. For another, it was accented—strangely. Not the way Yiqa's spoken words were accented. In Kila's mind this voice was all hard consonants and growls, yet she understood it perfectly.

You can feel me. Don't bother hiding.

Clop. Clop. Clop.

And then a hoof and bestial foreleg did emerge from the light. Kila saw the light was carried upon a fog. The hoof was horse-like but taller, tapering into a furred leg. The hem of a thick robe, black as the bottom of a closed coffin, draped at the weird creature's shin.

The cot shot into the air and smashed against the ceiling. The wooden frame splintered and fell around Kila and Ragin. The bedding fluttered across the room as if blown on a strong wind.

Ragin cried out and lunged to cover Kila's head with his own head and shoulders. Nax let out a shriek of terror.

Ragin's embrace suddenly pulled away from Kila, though he clawed to keep hold. His body rose into the air until he held only a fist full of her nightclothes. She looked up into his horror-stricken face. His pale complexion glowed in the green light. Her garment started to tear, and he finally released her. He flew upward, arms and legs splaying as an unseen force slammed him to the ceiling.

The mercus sang in Kila's body, a vibration of ice and fire.

Nax scrambled behind Kila, spitting and hissing.

Be calm, Beloved One, the creature said. Kila sensed it was talking to Nax. How she knew this, she had no idea. Nax fell silent.

Ragin shouted for Kila to run, his voice cracking and edged with the madness of panic. And no wonder. For standing over Kila was a monster.

From its hooves to its horrific head, it towered two and half spans—nearly twice Kila's height. The robes hung over massive shoulders. The arms dangled at the creature's side, ending in enormous hairy hands, each finger tipped with a black claw.

None of this caused Kila a fraction of the terror as its face did. A heavy brow protruded over deep eye sockets, which seemed to hold orbs of flame instead of eyes. The nose was bulbous, and hung over a slash of a mouth. Nostrils flared with every breath, which rumbled deep in the creature's chest. A mane of bluish-black hair swept back from its head. But instead of tumbling down the creature's back, it faded into wispy tendrils of blurry smoke, as if on fire.

If I were free to do as I wished, I would take you to be mine own, Kila Sigh. Alas. He stooped, putting a hand on her head. He stroked her as she might stroke Nax. The touch was ice. She recoiled, and an animal hiss escaped her lips.

His fingers contracted into a fist and he straightened, pulling Kila to her feet by her hair. By reflex she grabbed his wrist to ease the pull on her scalp. The flesh beneath the creature's robe did not give at all, as if it were made entirely of bone.

He set her on her feet. Her knees wobbled, threatening to give out, but the creature did not release her hair. She willed her knees to lock. "Let go of me. And put Ragin down."

The creature did not obey. It didn't react at all.

She repeated her command, this time projecting it through her thoughts. *Let go of me. Put my friend down.* The fiery eyes flamed a moment, then the hand released her. Ragin fell.

Kila lunged to break his fall, but she did not get there in time. Nax leapt out of the way as Ragin struck the floor. He did not move. Kila knelt by him, turned him over. A gash on the side of his head seeped blood, and his left arm was bent at an odd angle. She pressed her head to his chest, heard the rattle of breath.

She turned on the monster. *Why did you do that? He might die.* Her mercus vision arrowed into the creature, searching for the iron in his blood. The rage guided her thoughts. She would make ash of this beast.

But there was no iron in his blood. Or any other metal at all. Not even the clasp of the swirling patterned brooch at the throat of his robes was metal. The shape of the interleaving loops made her dizzy. She looked away.

Come, delicious one. Bring the Beloved with you.

I'm not leaving him like this.

The creature blew out a hard breath, making its nostrils flare. The eyes narrowed, and the greenish fire in them turned blue. *Heal him and let's be gone.*

I—I can't heal him.

Oh? Have you tried? Another chuckle, this one less menacing and more amused. *For one who sparks so brightly, I would think such a task the matter of a moment's concentration.*

Kila dropped to her knees next to Ragin. She felt the queller in her fist. She loosened her grip and found the ring had left deep indentations in her flesh. The ring was undamaged. She had no pocket in the nightgown, so she set the ring on the floor. Her mercus senses were alive to every sound and smell. The air even tasted of burnt hair now, making her tongue curl at the bitterness of it.

She saw the iron in Ragin's blood. The flow of it through his body was strong. His breath strained, though. She looked deeply into his chest, saw the blood pooling there. A section of one rib had splintered, puncturing something in his chest. Kila did not know the workings of the body's organs. She knew there were lungs there. Perhaps one had been pierced.

She saw all this, but no answer for it came to mind. Sending heat into his blood would accomplish nothing.

You truly have no skill with it, the beast marveled. *No wonder my master seeks you. What joy you will bring to him. Accursed be the bonds that keep me from taking you for mine own.*

Ragin coughed as he came awake. He hissed and moaned as the pain in his body came alive in his awareness. Blood trickled from his head, and a black bruise began to seep away from it, darkening his cheek and eye. His left one was swollen shut. More blood came from his nose.

The beast shoved Kila aside. *Observe.*

A new light came into existence between the creature's massive fingers. It cupped them, as if holding a ball. Then with slight side to side motions, he seemed to swirl it. The light was crimson, cut with streaks of black. *For me it is nothing, for I see deeply.*

Kila watched, fear momentarily forgotten. The mercus in the creature's hand was a whirl of sound and smell and flavor and color, heat and chill. She could not track it, could barely understand it. The pitches of high bells and deep drums rang and thrummed in her mind. Sharp smells like bitter tea and acrid sweat accompanied waves of heat and cold. All these she sensed, not only through her nose and eyes and skin, but also in the very center of her mind.

She blinked and leaned away. It was too much. An instantaneous headache made her wince and press her fingers to her temples.

The creature tilted its hand, spilling the crimson light onto Ragin's head wound. The boy sucked air through his teeth; his heels scrabbled over the floor. The beast doused Ragin's broken arm, and finally his torso. Each time the magical fluid touched the boy's body, he writhed in agony. But not a scream escaped his lips.

Now we go, the beast said into Kila's mind. She felt herself being lifted to her feet, again urged to stand by his pull on her hair.

She did not resist. Headache suddenly gone, her mind went blank, numbed by the miracle she had just witnessed. The flows of the mercusine had been as clear as the stitches of a master tailor: deft, quick, and deceptively simple. But also incomprehensible. She could repeat what she'd seen no more easily than she could tie the knots sailors fastened without so much as a thought for the twists and cinches their fingers worked.

Her mercus vision showed her that Ragin's

wounds were not only healed, but utterly reversed. He'd have no scar on his head, no ache in his arm, no trouble breathing. He was whole, as if he'd never been dropped three spans to a stone floor.

The beast guided her across the room. His chin suddenly jerked up and he scented the air in sharp sniffs. *They come. We must take a more direct way out.* Turning away from the door, he faced Kila's cot.

Again his hand began to glow, this time white. *Cover your ears.*

Kila obeyed, jaw slack as her mercus senses absorbed all that the monster did. The light also registered as sight and sound. Especially sound. A low throbbing that made her bones itch, her skull feel ready to explode. The beast thrust his palm against the wall. The brickwork shivered at his touch, blurring before Kila's eyes.

She watched the mercus at work, but comprehended little of what she saw or heard. A dissonance, like the clash of pipers playing all wrong—and yet holding together a frightening sort of melody— pounded in the chamber.

The surface of the brick flaked away in sheets of dust. Then more. And with a final hiss, a whole section of wall turned to sand and poured into the chamber. Amazingly, the rest of the wall stayed upright, leaving an oblong hole before them. The creature stepped through, beckoning to Kila.

Another shock. The opening led into a garden.

All this time, Kila had assumed her room was underground. She stepped through, more from amazement than willingness to follow the fearsome beast.

Why are you going? Nax sent.

Because he told me to. He—

It is dangerous. We should run.

Dangerous. The word hung suspended in her mind. There was no falseness in it. And yet, she only felt wonder. The scent of sweet spices and blossoms in the garden added to a sense of safety. Not danger. And the beast . . . Was it hideous? Or was it merely strange? Now that she could see him in the moonlight, see the regal green glow that emanated from him, she thought him magnificent.

A sharp sting on her ankle made her dance back. Nax retracted her claws and spat at Kila. *Run!*

The shock of her own cat striking her made Kila pause. In that fraction of hesitation, she caught the subtle smell in the air, an alluring spice that came not from the garden, but from the beast. He looked at her, arms crossed. His brow dipped over his eyes in a stern glare. *Come, delicious one.*

The smell increased. Kila remembered Goolsoy demonstrating the power of smell when used to enhance allure. It had encouraged Kila's predisposition to like him. This creature had overwhelmed her repulsion entirely. Only now that she sensed what he was doing did the charm break. Horror took its place.

Her bare feet slipped on the sand as she backed

away. *Begone, demayne!* she sent, crossing the fingers of one hand and tapping her ear with other.

Laughter. The creature raised a fist to the sky. The moonlight smeared, making the air shimmer as if heat rose from the beast. *Step close. We must away before she arrives.*

Kila felt the tug of his allure, but she shirked it off. A nightskirl called a warbling tune from the hedges that bordered this section of the garden. Fog rolled from the beast in billowing waves, washing around Kila's shins and pouring into the room where Ragin still lay. Nax leapt onto her cot to stay above it.

You will come. No attempt at allure. Kila's feet obeyed, though her mind rebelled. She stepped toward him, knees locked, shoulders tight. She had felt this compulsion once before.

Nax! I can't stop.

The fog . . .

Nax was stranded atop the cot. Ragin was hidden beneath the vapor.

The creature's slit of a mouth spread, showing a row of jagged teeth. One finger beckoned her forth, each jerk forcing a step from her body. She managed to turn her head away, but still she walked, taking stiff step after stiff step.

Nax! Tell Oly what happened to me. Tell him to make Wen take you away from here. Far away.

I can't leave you.

Nax!

The cat jumped from the cot and sprinted toward Kila. The small gray leapt from the fog, catching her claws in the front of Kila's nightgown. Each claw jabbed into Kila's skin, on her stomach, her breasts. Nax's teeth clamped on Kila's collarbone. Pain split Kila's consciousness. But she knew she needed it. She hugged Nax close.

The beast snorted like a bull. It stamped its hoof on the grass.

My delicious has fire. But she now has the Beloved. Let us go. He whirled his arms about his head. The fog rose, and around him a spiral of green light twisted like a water spout.

Something rammed into Kila, forcing her into the fog. Nax let go and scrambled away.

The beast roared with rage.

"Tenne yew wreet ivay!" The Voluptuary charged into Kila's room, an orb held aloft. It shone with pure white light that cut through the fog, dissipating it in an instant.

The creature roared and disappeared in a swell of green light.

2

———

WILLSHIFT

Ragin was on top of Kila. He crawled off her and collapsed onto his back. His chest heaved with the effort he'd expended tackling her.

"What in Ori's blessed bower is going on here?" This came from Sens Renna, who bustled past the Voluptuary to help Kila sit up. "I smell taint-tell."

"Demayne," the Voluptuary said in a low voice. She trudged through the mound of sand and came into the garden. After checking Ragin, she knelt next to Kila. "The queller, girl. Where is it?"

Mind clearing thanks to the crisp wintry air, Kila looked at her hand. Where had the ring gone? Then she remembered. "I set it next to Ragin after he fell off the ceiling."

"After he *what*?" Sens Renna said.

The Voluptuary got to her feet and went into the

room. She returned with the ring. "I told you never to remove it."

"But that—demayne. I had to fight it."

"Fight it? *Fight it?* Is that what you thought you were doing? I saw what Ragin did. He saved you from going with it, wherever it was bound." She shoved the ring onto Kila's finger. The world dulled, but Kila was thankful for it. The taste of the beast's stink vanished from her tongue.

The head of the Way of Ori stood once more. Kila noticed the orb she'd wielded was no longer in view. "Had you done as I commanded and kept the queller on your finger, the demayne would never have scented you out. By removing it, you showed yourself to him."

"Of what order was the beast?" Sens Renna asked.

The Voluptuary answered only with an odd look. Sens Renna said nothing more, but she wavered and her lovely complexion paled. "Let's get you two to another room."

Kila didn't resist as she was helped to stand and led down the hall to a novitiate's chamber almost identical to the last one. The Voluptuary summoned two strong novitiates to help move Ragin to his cot. She and Sens Renna lingered over the boy for a long time, conferring in soft voices. Kila couldn't hear them, and when she tried to join them she was sent back to her own cot with sharp stares.

When the two women finally condescended to look

at Kila again, they no longer had the air of disgruntled hens. "Ragin is well. If what you say is true, and the creature healed grave injuries, then he will require a day or two of sleep. The mercusine can guide healing, but it draws from the body's own stores of energy to do it."

Nax had curled up in Kila's arms and now slept as if nothing untoward had happened. Kila stroked the soft fur, drawing comfort from the cat's warmth and peaceful slumber. "I told you true. The demayne called me 'delicious one'. What does that mean?"

The Voluptuary's mouth pinched. "A vile thing for it to say, to even think. Turn your mind away from those taunts. Demayne use names in subtle ways. First to identify, then to lay claim. Given time, a demayne-bestowed name will have sway over your thoughts and actions. Who knows to what end? Reject the name. Do not give it power."

Kila did not understand any of what the woman had just said. "He complained that he couldn't make me his own. He was under the control of someone else. His master."

"I should hope so. If demayne could come here at will, and were free to do what they wanted, we'd all be enslaved. But to one powerful in the summoning arts, a demayne makes a deadly agent. I sense the Hargothe's hand in this."

"Surely not," Sens Renna said, pressing her hand to her chest. All the peacefulness the woman cultivated had shattered, exposing a brittleness Kila had never suspected. "The Way of Til would never tolerate such practices, even to further Til's glory."

The Voluptuary grimaced, her nostrils widening as some long-held suspicion was confirmed. "Serving Til has never been the Hargothe's purpose. And many Donse Masters follow his example, invoking the Father God's name as they extract money from the Radiants and abduct children from Terriside homes. Yes, there are good Donse Masters, just as surely as there are few wicked Sensuals. But the Hargothe is greedy for power. His mind is bent upon this girl, and now nothing will do but to have her."

Kila rubbed her cheeks and knuckled the corners of her eyes. She was both tired and alert. The combination was making her irritable. "How could a withered old man control a beast as huge as that? And the power! It smashed Ragin's cot against the ceiling. It turned brick to sand, and it took control of my body."

Each statement made Renna wince, and made the Voluptuary's already pinched mouth scrunch tighter. "Leave us, Renna."

The placid woman nodded in acquiescence and left.

A short, sturdy woman, the Voluptuary had a round, handsome face that matched the rest of her. Her hair, equal parts gray and black, was pulled away from her face. The sparkling headpiece she wore during the day must still be in her chambers.

"Where's Sens Goolsoy?" Kila asked, suddenly suspicious. "Where are those Iopsi women I saw the first day?"

"Sleeping, presumably."

"But you came from . . . wherever your room is, all the way down here. If you felt the demayne using the mercus, Goolsoy should have felt it, too."

"You make many incorrect assumptions, Kila Sigh. It is no wonder you are in constant trouble." The woman shifted her weight on the stool and fidgeted with the skirts of her night robe. "You said the demayne controlled your body. Tell me more about that."

"I fought it, but he made me walk toward him."

"I see. And how did you know the Hargothe was a withered old man?"

"You told me."

"I did no such thing. I have never seen him."

Kila knew because she had seen him, beyond the curtains of a sedan chair. She wasn't going to tell the Voluptuary about that. She did not trust the woman that much. "Maybe I filled in the details from my imagination. My father always said I had a creative memory." Kila laughed at the joke, but trailed off when the Voluptuary didn't join in.

"Who was your father?" the woman asked.

"Just a man who had a run of bad luck."

The conversation was starting to feel like the early stages of a fist-fighter bout, where each combatant danced, throwing soft, testing blows to see how their opponent would react. Kila knew the Voluptuary was probing for some detail, some piece of information that would complete a puzzle she'd been piecing together. But Kila had been taught—first by her father and then by Wen—that information was not free. "You want something, you have to give something," she said to the woman.

This did provoke a laugh, though one without much humor in it. "What do you want?"

"I want to leave this place. And your promise you won't have Yiqa drag me back by my hair."

"Even after what just happened here? Do you truly hate it here so much that you would risk death—or worse—just to be free of us?"

"You keep telling me how desirable my power is to everyone. Why would you be any different? I've lived in Cheapsgate my whole life. *Cheapsgate.* Do you think I'm innocent in the ways of people? Everyone uses everyone. Except for my family, I trust nobody. Now, you and Renna and Goolsoy seem like you want to treat me nice. But I've met a lot of longshoremen who smile and talk sweet just to get a girl into a dark corner where they can be free with their hands."

The Voluptuary sighed and patted her knees. "The force the demayne used on you is called willshift. One powerful in the mercus can impose his or her will on you, make you do what you do not wish to do. If the victim is also strong—like you—then willshift can be resisted. One weak—like Renna—may not know she has been willshifted at all. Among the Ways of the New Pantheon, willshift is forbidden. A demayne, however, will do whatever it wishes, for it is a creature of the Despised God." She leaned forward, eyes full of pity. "And now it knows you, Kila Sigh. Its master will almost certainly send it to find you again. But if not, such beings can act upon our world in indirect ways if determined to do so. If that demayne called you delicious, you may be assured it will never forget your name."

The Voluptuary stood and brushed her gown, as if talking about the Hargothe and demayne had dirtied her frock. "Sleep, if you can. Do not remove the queller—for all our sakes."

The woman swept from the room and closed the door softly behind her. Kila stared into the blackness of the room, arms wrapped around Nax. Ragin's soft breaths rose in the darkness.

The nagging instinct that had kept her awake had faded. Now she was left with her usual worries. Wen's sickness, Henley being the captive of the Hargothe, and her own imprisonment here.

But as she closed her eyes and sought sweet slumber, what played foremost in her mind was the magnificent workings of the mercus. The demayne had been fearsome and vile, but he'd woven the power of the mercusine like an artist. That such feats were possible intrigued her as much as frightened her.

Everyone said she was powerful in the mercusine. She had turned hundreds of thinnies to ash, though she hated to think of it. But the possibilities tantalized her. What might she do—what might she become—if she could learn even a tenth of what the demayne had showed her?

She didn't want much, just enough gold to set up as a legitimate recovery agent, the dream of her father. With such powers, recovery would be easy. The riches, great.

Smiling at the thought of it, she dozed. She awoke with her heart racing, brow wet with sweat.

Had she heard a raven cry, or had it been a dream? Just in case, she tapped her ears and said three times: "Die, raven, die."

3

———

ALLOW ME TO KILL

The disgraced Donse Master, Dunne Marlow, kept a small flat above a jeweler's shop. He spent most nights there these days, even though he owned a much larger home on the upper slopes of Terriside, where the sea breezes were fresher and didn't carry as much of the stink of the lower quarters.

At least the little flat was better than the drafty and damp abbey attached to the Cathedral of Til. Marlow had never liked the feel of that place. And the pressure of its location, in the shadow of the Divide, had always made him nervous and jumpy, as if the whole thing were about to fall upon him.

The jeweler's shop—a small, tidy front room with a few shelves and a steel vault in the back—was permanently closed. Marlow had purchased the building solely for its cellar.

Narrow, rickety stairs led down to the dank chamber, where a random assortment of jewelers' trade items were stashed.

Marlow patted these barrels and crates as he wound through them. Most were covered with a layer of dust. The jeweler had died long ago. Marlow supposed these things held some value, but he preferred no one to come down here. The entrance to the tunnel wasn't visible to untrained eyes, but he was a cautious man. No reason to tempt Pol into tripping a workman and have him fall through the false wall.

The cellar walls were stone, each piece the size of a fat pumpkin. But on the southeastern corner the stones were illusory. Marlow did not feel the mercus resonances that caused the illusion of the stone wall to exist. He rarely indulged in the mercus, for fear that his brother Tenn would feel him out. And now that Tenn was the Hargothe, there was worse than mere death at stake.

Marlow walked straight into the illusory stone, shivering as the chill crossed his body. Even having gone through hundreds of times, he could never avoid the terrifying thrill of that moment. Whether the feeling was a product of his imagination or an effect of the mercus at work, he did not know. In fact, he didn't have the first clue how such an illusion could be accomplished, much less how it maintained itself without someone actively powering the effect. Nor did he particularly care.

The tunnel wasn't long. It ended at a door. Marlow had long ago broken the lock. The door swung on its hinges without the slightest squeak. Beyond was the chamber. Magnificent and impossible. And dark.

Having shirked his studies while still an acolyte, Marlow could only speculate how such a vast space could occupy the world he knew was also there. Why, if he walked down the street and descended to any other cellar, he should come out somewhere in this same chamber. However, having done the experiment a number of times, he knew he wouldn't.

This chamber existed only beyond the illusory corner wall of the jeweler's shop. And that meant the portal took him . . . elsewhere. He grinned to think of it. Terrifying. Wonderful. Even better, the chamber held the only Derslin Wheel in Starside. And it was known only to Dunne Marlow.

To get to the wheel itself was a matter of walking through darkness. It didn't matter which direction he went.

He tore a flashtaper and set his whale-oil lantern alight. The glow spread across a smooth tile floor, forming an oblong circle of orange light. No light reached a ceiling. Marlow doubted there was one. A breeze ruffled his hair. He breathed it in, always interested to learn what new thing he might experience. Today the air carried the verdant and lush scent of a garden.

The walk usually took a quarter of an hour. He

moved slowly. Distance didn't matter here—only time. No reason to exhaust himself. He plodded along, the soles of his boots scuffing softly on the floor.

It was the floor that signaled his arrival, for the smooth grayness changed to a mosaic of tiles fitted into a swirling pattern. Marlow knew better than to study it too closely, for the design made him dizzy and nauseated. The forms flowed into each other in odd ways that made him feel like he was standing sideways.

He continued until his lantern illuminated the columns surrounding him. The Derslin Wheel had innumerable columns. Marlow had tried to make a complete catalog, reasoning that by starting at one, recording the symbol etched upon it, and then moving to the next, he would eventually make a complete circuit of the wheel and arrive back where he started.

Except it didn't work that way. He'd once left lanterns along the way so he could mark his progress. But some oddity in how distances or time worked brought him back to the second lantern, having never bypassed the first. And even then, the column next to the lantern was different from what he'd noted in his ledger.

A marvelous mystery was a Derslin Wheel. But Marlow had never been content to marvel when he could profit. What a Derslin Wheel could do interested him more than what it was.

Today he merely waited. It was not a long wait, for

at the center of the wheel, upon an area of the floor marked out by stones Marlow had placed, a green glow came into being. It intensified and swirled, higher and higher, bringing with it more of that garden smell. Marlow detected rose and apple blossom upon the air. Delightful.

Fog rolled from the light. Marlow loved seeing the appearance of his demayne. A marvel. A true marvel!

The demayne appeared, arms folded across its chest. Such a huge beast, at least nine feet tall and covered with a thick black robe. It wore the odd pendant at its throat, a smaller version of the floor mosaic.

Marlow's delight collapsed. He removed his amulet, twisting the leather cord around his thick fingers. With it removed, he felt the rush of the mercusine. Since he was *elsewhere*, he knew it was safe to tap into the subtle world without his brother probing into his mind. *Where is the girl, Flaumishtak?*

She remains at the Baths of the so-called Goddess Ori. We were interrupted by a woman wielding a bane-eye.

Marlow set aside his curiosity about the bane-eye. He'd never heard that term before. But it confirmed his suspicion that the Voluptuary had been collecting mercusine artifacts that rightly belonged to the Way of Til. *You confirm that you found Kila Sigh there?*

I do. Now pay me my due.

Marlow smiled and ambled to the perimeter of protection he'd established with the stones. There was nothing special about the stones themselves. It was the ritual surrounding them and the names he'd given them that mattered. Demayne were obsessed with names. It made them strong, but it also made them vulnerable. The trick was to do the naming before the demayne appeared in this world. Only in a Derslin Wheel could such be done with any degree of control or safety. And not much of the latter.

I shall pay you when you meet the terms of our contract. You hand the girl to me, you get what we agreed.

They will have placed wards over her chamber. I'll never get in now.

Wards. Interesting. Marlow knew a little about wards, but he doubted the Sensuals did. A conundrum, really. He didn't want to tell a demayne that few knew how to form mercus wards any more. On the other hand, his brother had promised him a position at the Citadel if he delivered the girl to him.

The demayne said, *If you allow me to kill those who interfere, it will go much easier. But I cannot defeat wards set against me. Not unless you release me from these stones.*

Never!

As for Marlow's prohibition on killing, that had been to protect himself on the off chance someone connected the demayne to him. The demayne was sworn not to reveal his master's name. But his brother knew of the connection. And the Hargothe might decide it was easier to have his brother arrested for consorting with a murderous demayne than to deliver his promised appointment to the Citadel. If there was no killing, there was no reason for the Hargothe to point his skeletal finger at Marlow.

Marlow sighed. Family was such a complicated mix of animosity and loyalty.

There are no wards, Flaumishtak. The Sensuals haven't the slightest idea how to form them. And to prove my conviction, I give you permission to utter my name if you are entrapped by one.

Utter your name? The beast snorted with derision. *What consolation would that be if I were ensnared?*

I would be dragged before a tribunal and then burned at the stake. Which is why you should accept my assurance that there are no wards.

The beast had little choice, and that was plain by its frustrated huffs and scowls. For a demayne to wander the world of men—even as constrained as it was—was a privilege few of them ever received. Upon returning to its own plane of hell, this demayne would be all the more powerful for the time it spent here.

There is another problem, the demayne said. *The girl is blocked from the mercusine by a queller. She wears it upon her finger. She is practically invisible to me. I only found her by sniffing out her Beloved One. Fear compelled her to remove it, else I would never have known her as the one you seek.*

A queller. That was very interesting. The Sensuals must have given it to her. Sneaky. The Voluptuary played a dangerous game withholding such objects of power from the Way of Til. The laws agreed upon at the synod of the New Pantheon were unambiguous on that point. Til the Father stood above all others. All His artifacts were to be remanded to the Way of Til.

So the Voluptuary had something called a bane-eye, and a queller. What else did she have? A question for another time, but at least he had gleaned information he might trade for a favor or two.

The girl and her cat, alive, he said. *I grant you two lives to take as you see fit, as long as it is in service of your mission. No Donse Masters may be harmed, nor anyone in the Citadel.*

Flaumishtak bowed slightly. Not an act of deference so much as an acknowledgement of the rules.

The swirl of green light flared then dissipated. The demayne vanished, leaving only the stink of burnt hair behind.

4

SHE UNDERSTOOD DEBT

Kila's clothes—boy's trousers and a square-necked top, both charcoal—were set out for her when she woke that morning. Someone had cleaned them of the ash and filth she'd picked up in the thinnies' cavern city. Kila still felt the top was too snug and a tad too short, but she preferred it to the novitiates' robes. At least the pants she'd stolen had pockets.

The queller ring was in one of them now, and the zing was upon her.

The Rose Hall was awash in color as the rising sun shone through the Sunrise Rose window. She smelled the tea Sens Goolsoy had again spilled on his robes. She felt the texture of the tiles beneath her bare feet. Before her, the door stood impervious and uncaring.

The keyless lock mechanism revealed its metal tumblers, but nothing else. As for moving any of them

. . . she accomplished nothing. Sens Goolsoy said her feat with the iron in blood was unlike anything done by a single person—or a group—in known history. "Perhaps ancients do such feat," he'd said. "So much lost now."

When she told him how she had pulled nails from the box holding Nax beneath the lake, he had stammered in shock. He had demanded she show him by placing a copper plug on a table before her. "Move plug."

She'd had no idea how to move it, and now she had no idea how to move the tumblers. But his words had proved something to her. She turned to face him. The Voluptuary had joined them, too. Kila had heard her come in, had recognized her smell. "No one has ever opened this door, have they?"

"Not in my lifetime," the Voluptuary said.

"I've heard of Donse Masters move object," Goolsoy said. He pressed his thumb and forefinger close together. "Small one. Not even nail."

Kila remembered the desperation she'd felt when she'd used the mercus to destroy her enemies. Nax had been drowning. Kila had merely acted. She hadn't thought about what she was doing.

"You must train with Sens Goolsoy," the Voluptuary said. "For your safety and that of everyone around you."

Kila slipped the queller onto her finger. The zing cut off. "You say that as if I have a choice."

The woman's jaw set. Her jeweled hairpiece sparkled and flared as the sunlight grew brighter. "I'd prefer you choose to stay, because then your mind will be fully engaged on your learning. If you prefer to go and I keep you here, you will only think of escape."

"That's true. So I choose to go."

Goolsoy's face fell. "No. Must stay!"

The Voluptuary came very close to Kila, took her hands. "Someone brought a demayne into this world to hunt you. It is safer here than anywhere else."

"It made a hole in a brick wall and disappeared in a flash of green smoke. How in Kil's name can you protect me from that?"

"Do not speak of the Despised God under this roof," the woman snapped. "The incident last night was regrettable, but that was because I did not foresee such an incursion. Now that we know a demayne is loose, we can set wards against it. And we could teach you to set wards."

"And how long will that take?"

"Year. Maybe two," Goolsoy said. "Maybe day."

"Maybe never," Kila said. "Look, I have important things to do. People out there need me."

"Your brother's medicine will be assured if you stay," the Voluptuary said. "Perhaps we could bring him to the baths. Protect him, too."

The offer startled Kila. Her eyes narrowed in suspicion. If the Ways of Til and Pol wanted her, then Kila had to assume the Way of Ori had their own designs on her power. Goolsoy's eagerness to see how she'd used the mercus might be mere curiosity, or it might be hunger for the power himself. And the Voluptuary's generosity could merely be a different path to the same end. By being generous and offering Kila her freedom, the woman sought to lure Kila into serving her purposes. Whatever they were.

Kila's father had been cynical. He often said there was nothing men wanted more than power over other men. And nothing the powerless wanted more than to pull down those with power over them. What Kila wanted was to be with Nax and her brother and the boys. She wanted to go back to her life and find a way to start up the recovery business her father had dreamed of. That was it.

And she understood debt. The more she came to rely on the Sensuals, the more she would owe them.

"Thank you for having Finta make my brother his tincture," Kila said to the Voluptuary. "And thank you for taking care of me and Nax. I won't forget that."

Resignation tightened the Voluptuary's face. "You may return here to train any time."

"I may. Someday. But there are things I have to take care of." Rescuing Henley being the most important.

"Never remove the ring. Travel armed." The Voluptuary waved forward a Sensual, who handed her a bundle. The woman gave it to Kila. Inside the fabric was Cayne, her father's blade. "Yiqa has offered to train you in the ways of combat."

"Now *that* I will happily accept."

The Voluptuary dismissed her, and Sens Renna guided Kila through the doorway behind a huge tapestry on the rear wall. How the woman made the doorway appear, Kila could not see or feel due to the queller on her finger. Renna led Kila through a series of corridors to a simple wooden door. It opened into the public baths where Kila and Ragin had come after the disaster with the thinnies.

Kila realized she hadn't said goodbye to Ragin. "Tell Ragin I release him from his vow." She didn't need the hapless boy getting killed trying to find her in Cheapsgate. She paused a moment, considering whether she should go down to the ward and tell him herself.

But the thought of his eyes on her, and the odd discomfort she knew the meeting would provoke, made her think better of it. Better for him to be far away from her, especially with all the bad people who wanted her. She'd seen him nearly get killed by the demayne. She didn't think she could bear witnessing that again. It was better for both of them to make a clean parting.

Sens Renna seemed shocked by the suggestion. "It isn't up to you to forgive the vow. The vow was made to Ori."

"But he can't come after me. And he will if you don't release him from that silly vow."

"He cannot leave without the Voluptuary's permission."

"We did it before."

"There will be a fire in the library fireplace henceforth."

That would do it. She and Ragin had climbed up the chimney to escape the novitiates' ward the last time. "So he's going to be forced to break his vow. That seems rather cruel."

Renna's peaceful face betrayed no sense of unfairness. "He misinterprets the vow. I shall counsel him on how to do penance, and how to fulfill his promise within the restrictions placed upon him."

Kila had gotten to know the boy during their escape and adventure in the thinnie tunnels. She was not at all convinced that Ragin would accept Renna's perspective. But Kila decided that was Renna's problem. She had other things to attend to.

With a tight smile and a nod, she bade Sens Renna goodbye. Then she was out the front door and onto the Street of the Diadem. Sunshine and a blue sky greeted her. Once she got to the roofway she found Nax waiting, tail curled primly around her little white feet. The cat had regained some of the weight she'd lost following her drowning, but she still looked emaciated to Kila.

Let's find some food, Kila sent.

Nax meowed in agreement.

5

WRETCHED HIVE

The pair of them kept to the roofway until dropping to pass through the sewers to Cheapsgate. They stopped for a bowl of Josef's chowder. He didn't blink when Kila asked if he had any scraps that didn't make it into his pot. Nax fed well.

She found Wen and Oly in a back room of Critt Sanglo's tavern. As it was still morning, nobody but Critt was around. The proprietor was contentedly smoking a pipe and leaning back in a chair. His hair was pulled back into a sailor's queue and tarred black.

Critt watched Nax nose around the tables. The man shook his head and made a ward with his pinky. Anyone else in Cheapsgate would snatch the cat up and bolt for the cathedral. But Critt had known Kila's father, owed his life to him, in fact. In return, he watched out for Wen and Kila. He was the closest thing to an ally they had. Also, he hated Donse Masters.

Wen leaned against the bar, a cup of water before him. He was pale and thin. He greeted Kila with a wan smile and an uncharacteristic hug. "Thought we'd lost you," he said.

"Thought the same 'bout you. Where's Fallo?"

"The Warren. He's been taking care of Huff. The cat's still alive but rarely wakes up."

"No sign or word about Henley?"

He shook his head and downed his water. "Let's go." He dropped a silver plug on the bar. "Thanks, Critt Sanglo. You're a good man."

The huge proprietor squinted and looked all around, as if there might be eavesdroppers. "Hush that talk. Word might get 'round."

Kila and Wen found Fallo in the den. Four paces by four and furnished with sleeping pallets and dust, the den had been Kila and Wen's home for the better part of the last year.

The cries of small children and a scolding mother came through the rough floorboards. This space—once a warehouse—was never meant to be living quarters. The fish-oil lamp burned on one wall, sending up a tentacle of black smoke. Huff lay in a pile of rags Fallo had scavenged from Kila's sleeping pallet. Lop was curled next to him, also asleep.

Fallo leaned his back to the wall, knees up. He'd been studying a small slip of paper when they came in. He quickly stuffed it into his jacket pocket and helped Wen get seated.

Nax nosed Huff's ear and gave it a tentative lick. *He's not there.*

Kila stroked Huff's orange fur, felt his warmth. *Naxie, you were like this when I woke up.*

The little gray had no response to this. She didn't remember much about her drowning ordeal, and any questions about it were met with a revival of the panic she'd experience in the box.

Kila said, "Did you both see the vision of the old man and the two acolytes of Til?"

Fallo's single black eyebrow lowered over his eyes. "The vision from Henley? Yes."

Wen nodded, lips pressed tight. He stared at Huff, eyes soft with pity. He coughed into the crook of his elbow.

"I think he was at the Abbey," Kila said. "The Donse Masters have him. They did something to him. Something so painful it passed to Huff, who passed it to our cats, who sent it to us." She looked at Fallo, who had an unusually serious expression on his villainous face. "What did you see when they took him?"

"I wasn't with him. I didn't see a Kil-damned thing. Not until that vision hit me."

They were all quiet for a time. Something had been bothering Kila, a piece of unfinished business with the Warren landlord Parlo Odok and his thug Jocko. "Parlo didn't sell me out to Yiqa. He and Jocko were taking me somewhere else. To someone else. I don't know who. Then Yiqa rescued me from Jocko, in a way."

Wen's eyes met hers. They were clearer than she'd seen them in a long time thanks to a strong dose of Finta's medicine. Though he looked weak, she saw the man in his face now, as if all boyishness had been drained from him. What remained was angular. Like Father. "Who was Parlo taking you to, then?" he asked.

Kila had an idea about that. "The Voluptuary mentioned someone called the Hargothe. He can feel the potential for mercus in people. He serves the Way of Til. A kind of Donse Master, I guess. I think that's who Henley saw."

She toyed with the queller ring. The Hargothe was out there now, yearning for her, if the Voluptuary was to be believed. "That means we need to get into the Abbey somehow."

They sat in silence. The ridiculousness of going into the Abbey—especially with cats—didn't need pointing out. Kila said, "Didn't Father mention knowing a defrocked Donse Master?"

Wen lay back on his pallet, clasping his hands behind his head. "I remember that story. Dunne Sik. He was an Erilen. But he was old when Father knew him. Surely he's dead now."

"You want to talk to a Donse Master?" Fallo said. "I know the most powerful one of them all. Highest

Binel." His face was dark, angry. Losing track of Henley had robbed the boy of much of his humor.

"I thought the Highest was Nare Chilow," Wen said.

"He was deposed. Rumor is that he was discovered to have a consort among the Spinsters of Pol."

"How do you know the new one?" Kila asked.

Fallo didn't answer right away. A war waged across his face. Both sides were dark and full of anger. Finally he said, "Binel is my uncle on my mother's side."

Kila laughed. So Fallo had retained some of his humor after all. "This isn't time for joking. If we want Henley back, we have to get into the Abbey. I could probably sneak in. But I wouldn't have the first clue where to look. If we were invited in, at least we'd have a chance to poke around. Maybe ask some innocent questions."

"I was not making sport, Kila Sigh. Highest Binel is family."

Wen sat up. Kila leaned toward Fallo. "Look me in the eyes and tell me true."

Fallo locked his black eyes on hers. "I tell you true. But there is a problem."

"What?"

"If my uncle sees me, he may turn me over to my father. And then Father will finish me off." He drew a finger across his throat. "There's a reason I'm living in

Cheapsgate, lass, and it isn't merely to ogle pretties like you."

Kila scrunched her nose. "That is . . . unfortunate. But maybe there's a way to use your connection. Somehow."

The rug door pushed in. A woman in black oozed into the den. Yiqa, the Voluptuary's Alnassi stealth killer. Her intense eyes swept the small space for threats. A wisp of her white hair escaped her hood. On most women, it would speak of advanced years. In a confrontation with Yiqa, such an assumption would be a deadly mistake.

Yiqa pointed a slender finger at Kila's face. "Comme witt mee. Beginnn trainink.

Kila had fought the woman twice and had lost in embarrassing fashion both times. "Now?"

"Enemeez do nottt waaiit, so you mussst nott wait."

Kila was tired. But learning from Yiqa was one thing she would not pass up. She looked back at Fallo and her brother as she lifted the rug door. "I'll be back in one wink of Ori's lusty eye. I want ideas. How do we get into the Abbey?"

Yiqa led Kila through the maze of narrow passages, walls made of whatever scrap materials the denizens of the Warren could find. Doors were rugs, strings of beads, planks bound with rope, or non-existent.

The fumes of fish-oil lamps and fry pans left a haze of acrid smoke in the air. Elderly ladies sat in open doorways, knitting, gossiping and sipping hard black tea. Children ran amok, shrieking, half-naked and filthy. Men sulked, shoulders drawn down like wary animals.

Kila barely noticed them, but Yiqa waded through it all as if she were about to attack everyone.

They descended nearly vertical stairs—more akin to ladder-rungs than steps—and went to the front of the Warren. Yiqa stopped at Parlo Odok's office and motioned for Kila to go in. The landlord was tied to a chair, a filthy cloth gag tied around his face. Upon seeing Kila, his eyes widened and he shook his head.

It seemed Yiqa had anticipated one of Kila's planned stops. "Who paid ya ta kidnap me?" Kila asked.

Yiqa pulled the gag away. Odok heaved in deep breaths, spittle dribbling down his chin. "A woman. Plump. Pretty."

"Not a Donse Master?"

"D'ya have wax in yer ears? I just said a plump woman!"

Yiqa smacked him upside the head. Parlo squealed like a swirehog.

"What'd she look like?" Kila said. "Details."

"Brown locks. I don't make a habit o' lookin' at a lass's face when other parts o' her be more enticin'."

"Thiss mann disgussts mmmee."

"Coming from Odok, that was a compliment," Kila

said. "When ya had Jocko grab me, ya said someone was payin' ya five gold skillets for me."

"Aye. Bright 'n shiny as th' day, they be. Fresh minted ravens." Skillets issued by Her Enlightened were minted with her seal: The Raven-in-Flight.

"Tell Jocko ta show me where ya were takin' me afore Yiqa slapped ya both senseless."

"You tell 'im."

Yiqa smacked Odok's head again, making a cracking noise resound from his barren office walls. He yelped and snot came from his nose. Sobbing he said, "Aye! Aye. Jocko will take ya. And Kil be done with ya both."

Yiqa released Odok from his bindings. "Kila Sssigh and herr fffamily arre safffe frommm you." There was no question in her statement. Parlo nodded so vigorously his neck made popping noises. Rubbing his wrists, he scurried to the entrance where Jocko stood.

Jocko was a bull-shouldered mountain, chest stretching the fabric of his dingy tunic. He was as stupid as he was huge, but his loyalty to Odok was unbreakable. Nobody knew why.

Sighting Yiqa, the huge thug lunged for the club leaning against the wall. But Parlo interposed his own body between Jocko and the Alnassi woman. "Avast hoistin' that skull-crusher, Jocko. Take Kila an' her, uh, friend to th' place we discussed."

Jocko's thick face bunched and turned bright red. Kila found his curses creative and amusing, but Yiqa glared at him. Jocko wilted before the woman, his throat apple bobbing as he swallowed.

"Lead on, Jocko," Kila said.

Nax was nowhere in sight, but Kila felt the small gray slinking about on the rooftop.

Jocko climbed a stack of crates and set off across the roofs of Cheapsgate. Kila and Yiqa followed.

It took ten minutes. The destination did not surprise Kila beyond the realization she should have guessed it. A rambling complex of shacks, all connected by mismatched chunks of ship wreckage. Smoke plumed from chimney pipes here and there. The place did not possess a front entrance. Rather it was a neighborhood unto itself, with hundreds of entrances.

Kila dismissed Jocko, who mumbled curses as he turned back toward the Warren. Yiqa did not move, so Jocko gave her a wide berth.

"Watt eess theeess place?"

"You'll never find a more wretched hive of villainous scum," Kila said. "This is Dox Viller's place. A tavern, brothel, inn, and prison all in one. And Dox . . . imagine Parlo Odok in Jocko's body. Let's go back to the den."

"You geeve up?"

"No. I don't *geeve* up. I'm not going in there, is all. Father told me and Wen many times to never, ever, ever go into Dox Viller's domain. If someone in there paid Parlo to turn me in, Dox knows about it. He's got fingers in everything, from Radiant houses to the Westbunk to the Donse Masters' privies. Probably has ears in the Citadel."

"Eef he iss ssoo powerffful, thenn why iss hee here?"

Kila shrugged. "He likes it, I guess."

They returned to the Warren. Kila decided to use the secret entrance on the outside of the den, so she went up to the long uneven roof of the warehouse. No reason to let Parlo or Jocko know all her comings and goings. Besides, she trusted Parlo's greed more than Yiqa's threats, which meant he'd turn her over to the highest bidder if he thought he could get away with it.

Nax emerged from a hidey-hole on the rooftop and rubbed against Kila's shin. She sent a welcome purr into Kila's mind. As Kila stooped to pick up her cat, a soft blow to the back of her knee sent her onto her backside. Nax scurried away.

Yiqa stood over Kila. "Now you trenn to fffight."

It took Kila a moment to realize Yiqa meant *train*. "Now?"

In answer, Yiqa's foot swung toward Kila's head. She ducked in time. Which meant Yiqa hadn't intended the blow to connect. Needing no further encouragement, Kila clambered to her feet.

Yiqa stood strong, shoulders back, eyes intent. "Bee mmy mirrorr." Knees bent, feet planted yet light upon the roof of the Warren, she moved in slow, fluid thrusts. Kila did her best to mirror the movements.

Soon, sweat coursed from her hair into her eyes, down her back, and soaked her clothes. Yiqa betrayed no signs of exertion.

She moves like a cat, Nax observed, sending approval through the bond.

And then the sparring began. An hour later, Kila descended the side of the Warren and slipped into the den through the secret door. Once inside, she collapsed onto her pallet. The boys questioned where she'd gone and why she looked so knackered.

"When Yiqa decides to train you, she trains the Kil-lovin' blood outta yer pores."

"We have an idea about how to get into the Abbey," Fallo said. "And we don't need to know any particular Donse Master to get us in."

Kila perked up, but she didn't move. "Well?"

"We take them a cat," Wen said.

Now she did sit up. "Have you two been trezzing it up while I've been getting my skull broke open?"

"No," Fallo said with a bit too much heat. Kila knew he had a small flask of the liquor on him at all times. He didn't seem to overindulge, which was lucky for him. She had no patience for drunkenness in her crew.

"Wait a Kil-damned minute. You're not thinking of turning in Startle, are you?" The black and white fuzzball with the constant look of surprise on its face was unbonded, and rarely showed his whiskers in the den. Nax said Startle was very stealthy and quite skilled at killing rats.

"No. Huff has volunteered."

Kila hadn't noticed the orange cat sitting near Wen. The cat didn't look too clever, but at least he was awake.

"Has Huff said how Henley is doing? Or where he is?"

"Huff doesn't know. Henley is too far away. Huff only knows he's alive."

"But the Donse Masters will kill Huff."

"Not if he just happens to get loose in the Abbey by mistake. Think about it. He's the perfect spy. If he can find a place to hide, he can sneak around by night. And he'll be able to talk to Henley once he's close enough."

It sounded like wool-headed plot to Kila, but it had one advantage: It was the only idea they had. "He won't be able to rescue Henley by himself."

"No," Wen said. "But Huff can talk to our cats, and they can talk to us. At least we'll have more information before we try to go in."

"When do we do it?"

"Tonight. After dark."

Finally, a plan. "Good. Now if you two will please be quiet, I am going to sleep."

But she couldn't sleep. *Nax, where is Startle?*

Nax curled onto Kila's chest. *That way.* She pointed her face north.

What is he doing?
Looking.
For what?
Someone.
Who?
Someone.

Kila knew better than to ask the same question. Nax was sending a ruffle of irritation about the entire conversation. She was tired, too. In fact, Nax was sending sleepiness into Kila's mind. For once, she welcomed the feeling.

6

RIGHT TO FEAR HER

The air in the Hargothe's cell was too cold. He rang the bell, four sharp clanks, signaling to the acolyte on duty to warm things up. The young man used his mercus skill—along with a heller—to heat water that ran in channels through the Hargothe's dark crypt chamber. The sound of water flow began instantly.

The Hargothe had been thinking about the heller—and objects like it—quite a lot recently. Artifacts of the mercusine were rare and not well understood. They focused and magnified certain mercus skills. Unassisted, the acolyte in the next room could heat a thimble of water to boiling in ten minutes. The effort would leave the lad exhausted and useless for a day. But the heller—a simple cube of iron—allowed the lad to heat hundreds of gallons with the same effort.

The Hargothe's sensitivity to the mercusine web

surpassed that of anyone else in the Abbey. He enjoyed communing with the subtle world. It resonated through him, appearing as lights and colors, sounds and flavors. Sometimes even as smells and textures.

The heller remained an utter mystery to him. He sensed the acolyte's effort, and he felt the result of it as warm water heated his room. But the heller itself was invisible to his mercus senses. It shouldn't be so, but it was. The whole question irritated him, so he usually avoided thinking of it. The girl's disappearance from the mercus reminded him of the absence of the heller.

Which reminded him of Dunne Marlow's silence upon the mercusine. Had Kila Sigh learned Marlow's trick? The idea made the Hargothe's guts burn. She was already too powerful.

"Why did you put her here, Til?" he whispered. It was a spontaneous utterance, one without precedent. The Hargothe did not believe in prayer, for it supposed the Father God was like man, with ears and a mind full of thoughts. That couldn't be. No, Til was the source of the mercusine, which made him more of an idea than a being. Til was Rightness. His teachings were a constraint on the wildness of mankind, who would behave like animals without his strictures.

And yet the Hargothe's question remained. Why did Kila Sigh exist? The girl had appeared upon the mercusine with no forewarning, not the least premoni-tion. He was a seer; he should have foreseen her coming. He could have scooped her up as a babe, raised her within the confines of the Abbey to serve his will.

The Nares were right to fear her. She outclassed them all in pure power. Should she harness that potential, truly gain mastery over it, could any stand against her? The Hargothe doubted it. Which was why he had to have her.

He rang his bell and waited for his elderly servant to bustle in. "Yes, Seer Hargothe?"

"I wish to speak with Her Enlightened Majesty."

"Seer?"

"I will go to her, of course. Pass my wishes to Highest Binel. He can arrange it."

"Yes, Seer." The man shuffled out, the sweat of his nervousness lingering in the room long after he left.

The Hargothe had never met the Enlightened. He supposed she did not even know if he truly existed. Many centuries had passed since the last Hargothe had died. His own awakening as a seer had come as a shock to the Donse Masters around him. It hadn't been a surprise to him. He had sought such power, worked diligently to cultivate his mercusine senses. But it hadn't been until the summoning of a demayne that his total power had been unleashed.

The toll his powers took upon his mind and body was a steep price. How much longer could he live in this frail shell? A year? Perhaps two?

Once he was done with the Enlightened, he would

turn his attention to the boy Henley. The Beloved One bonded to him was intriguing. Long had the Hargothe sought such a creature to bond to. If the boy's mind could be made more compliant, perhaps the Hargothe could satisfy several desires at once. A strengthened body, a Beloved One, and freedom from these crypts.

7

HOME IN HIS HEART

Winter had arrived. Snow fluttered from the black sky to settle on the cobblestone streets, where it turned into a thick slush. The roofway was treacherous in such weather, and though Kila's bare feet were tough, she was not used to having her toes submerged in the half-thawed mush of snow and water.

"We need to secure some foul-weather gear," Fallo said. Even in shoes and jacket, he shivered more than Kila. "I wouldn't mind a nice house on Quast Street. Also, a plump maid and a skilled cook to round out the household. I'll take the master suite, of course. You two can sleep down the hall, each in your own room."

Kila flashed her teeth at his attempt at humor. His fantasy was no surprise to her since she'd learned he'd come from money. While she wouldn't mind having a house of her own, she didn't like the idea of having servants constantly snooping around her abode. What a terrible invasion that would be. As for foul-weather gear, she wouldn't refuse it if Kil himself ascended from the fiery pits to dress her.

Wen coughed into the crook of his arm. She'd argued that there was no reason for him to come on this mission, but he'd ignored her. He hadn't even been able to run the roofway, for his legs were too unsteady to make the longer jumps. His eyes were bright, but not with the usual eagerness when starting a caper. He looked feverish.

They stood overlooking Dunne Medow Plaza, the vast stretch of flagstone that marked the main meeting point between Terriside and Gristenside. Along the Divide, abutting the Starside wall, stood the Cathedral of Til, pinnacles stretching heavenward. Wide steps led up to the great entry. Stretching to either side were the long buildings of the Abbey, where the Donse Masters and acolytes did whatever such people did. Mostly thinking up ways to meddle in people's affairs, Kila imagined.

The plaza itself was well-lit by mercus lights posted along the periphery and among the statuary in the central fountain. The plaza was empty.

The cats huddled together nearby, Huff at the center. The whole way from Cheapsgate, Nax, Lop, and even Oly had stayed close to Henley's orange cat, making sure he kept up. Whatever had happened to

Henley—whatever was still happening to him—it had an effect on Huff. But according to Nax, Huff could explain none of it.

Anything from Huff? she sent to Nax.

Henley is in there. Nax looked at the Abbey.

We knew that already. Can Huff talk to him from here?

No.

"So how does one collect the bounty?" Fallo said, rubbing his elbows and stamping his feet. "Do we just go to the front door and knock?"

"There is a side entry to the right," Wen said. "It is open all hours. A Donse Master is on duty to receive those in need."

"To receive their coin, you mean," Kila said. At least the Sensuals didn't charge for their services, though they did expect service in return.

Fallo recited: "And whosoever needs my comfort, seek it in My house. For My door is never closed to those who put Til above all others and glorify Me with coin."

"From the Theb. Although I think you added that bit about coin," Wen said.

"Let's go, then," Kila said.

"Not you. Not you either, Fallo. Both of you are too recognizable. I'll go."

Kila did not like this idea at all. Wen was shivering. "You shouldn't even be out in this weather. Let me do it. I have the queller, so they won't feel the mercus in me. Besides, the last person they'd expect to show up at their door is the girl they're looking for."

"It's warm in there," Wen said. "Since I'm sick, I should be the one to go in." He flashed a grin, then scooped up Huff. Oly, sodden and miserable, stomped after Wen as he slunk away to descend to the street. A minute later Wen crossed the plaza, the pitiful Huff in his arms.

"I've got a bad feeling about this," Fallo said as Wen climbed the steps to the Cathedral. He had moved as close to Kila as he dared, trying to share her warmth. She didn't mind, as long as he didn't get any ideas. That was something her father had warned her about. Boys were always getting ideas.

Wen was a tiny figure in the distance now. His head turned toward Kila and Fallo and he paused, then he went to the side door and disappeared inside.

Nax, where's Oly?

Under something, staying dry.

Tell him to tell you what is happening with Wen.

Oly says Wen is inside.

Kila suspected Oly's response was meant to irritate her. But one thing Nax had said made sense. "Let's get somewhere dry," she said to Fallo. The plaza was empty, and a sheltered cloister fronted the buildings opposite the Cathedral. Kila led Fallo down, the cats riding on their shoulders. From ground-level the Cathedral loomed high above, imposing and full of menace. Kila hated the grotesque gargoyles, mouths open to vomit snow melt. It was a building that didn't belong, an addition by man to a city that could have been beautiful. She wondered what the race who had constructed the city would think of the Cathedral.

Now sheltered in the cloister, Kila and Fallo hung back in the shadows of a column. It wasn't much warmer here, but the ground was dry. Kila's father had taught her that warmth of body began with warmth of thought. He sometimes went out to lie in winter snow, laughing at the weird looks of passersby. Using the mental technique he'd taught her, Kila imagined heat spreading from her abdomen to her hands and feet. It helped a little, but if she didn't get inside soon her feet were going to turn blue.

Please ask Oly to tell us what is happening with Wen.

Oly says Huff got loose and that the Donse Masters are hunting for him.

What about Wen?

Wen is coughing and lying on the floor. Oly is angry at you for letting Wen go in and doesn't want to tell you anything else.

"Come on, Fallo." Kila left the cloister and sprinted across the plaza. Fallo's footstep sounded behind her. "This isn't part of the plan," he said.

"Why do you always talk about plans?" Kila ran up the steps, breath billowing in the chill air. She found the side door and pushed in. A wave of warmth engulfed her.

Fallo stumbled in after her, uttering blasphemies

about the cold. He bumped into Kila who stood still, trying to absorb what was happening in the entry foyer. Wen lay on a reception desk, body convulsing, lips red with blood. Two men in acolyte's robes were holding him down. Shouts resounded just beyond another door. That had to be where the main Cathedral nave was.

One of the acolytes turned to see who had barged in. Kila recognized his face from Henley's vision. She didn't remember drawing Cayne, but the blade was suddenly in her grip. "Let him up."

"It's her!" With a cry the man lunged for her, arms spread wide. Surprise froze her for a moment, but instinct took over. She thrust Cayne forward. The razor-sharp point passed through robe and flesh, glanced off a rib, and found a home in his heart. His momentum carried him forward, driving her to the floor. Fallo shouted something, and the other acolyte answered with a shriek.

The dead acolyte rolled off her. Fallo stood above her, hideous and pale. "Well, get up!"

She obeyed, and together they took Wen's arms and dragged him into the cold. His coughing did not let up and his legs could barely help. They got him back to the colonnaded cloister, where he collapsed onto his back. Kila searched his pockets and found a pouch with Finta's tincture. She took a pinch and shoved it into his mouth. "Swallow it."

He choked on it. More spittle came from his mouth, tinged black from blood and Finta's herbs.

"They're coming out," Fallo warned. Across the plaza, a throng of acolytes and Donse Masters poured from the Cathedral's main entry.

There was no way to get Wen to the rooftops when he couldn't even stand. The desperation Kila had felt in the thinnie cavern was returning. She looked at the two escape routes available. The Harridan Gate led downslope, deeper into Terriside. But she didn't see how she could get Wen all the way back to the Warren. The Trialti Arch was at the other end of the colonnade. And there was help that way. "I have to ask you a favor," Kila said to Fallo.

"Does it involve me dying for no reason?"

"No. It involves you escaping. Go through the Harridan. Stagger and cough the whole way, make them think you're Wen. Lead them on Kil's Wild Hunt."

"What about you and Wen?"

"I'm going to take him to the Baths of Ori. Now go!"

Fallo tilted his head toward the Trialti Arch. "You going to carry him all by yourself?"

"Yes. Go!"

Fallo stumbled away, hacking and coughing, toward the Gate. Kila crouched by Wen in the shadows, watching the Donse Masters and acolytes fan across the plaza. One elderly man cried out and pointed at Fallo as he entered the darkness of the Harridan. As one, their heads turned. Like a flock of birds they swept after him, robes flapping behind them as they ran. A few stayed behind, grouped together to confer.

"All right, Wen," she said to her brother, "let's get you out of here."

8

ALWAYS HUNGRY

Wen was unconscious, thankfully. The coughing had stopped, but his breath came in labored wheezes.

He was a head taller than Kila but thin as a rail from his prolonged illness. Even so, she struggled to get his limp form sitting upright. Squatting, she flopped him over her shoulder. She strained under his weight as she stood, one arm around his legs, the other extended for balance.

Nax, tell Oly to stay behind us. If anyone follows, he should to try to lure them away.

No response came for several moments. *Oly says you should hurry.*

Kila started down the colonnade, slipping from shadow to shadow. The throng of Donse Masters was three hundred paces away, and wholly focused on their conversation. She entered the Trialti and passed to Gristenside.

From here it was a long trek upslope. She had the choice to take the winding Street of the Diadem or a shortcut up steep stairways. The former would take longer and increase her risk of being spotted by the Watch. They would be suspicious of a girl carrying an unconscious boy, especially when both were Cheapsgaters. She chose the stairs, though her thighs burned with every step.

Behind her, the bells of the Cathedral of Til began to sound.

No one follows, Nax sent. *Lop says Fallo is leading the Donse Masters in circles.*

What about Huff?

Hiding in the Cathedral. Nothing from Henley.

Good. Meet me at the Baths.

Nax would take a route along the roofs and probably beat Kila there.

Tromping boots sounded ahead. The Street of the Diadem was flanked by shops here. The pavement was broad and covered with a sheen of slush. Mercus lights shined atop posts set every fifty paces. Gristenside was very rich indeed.

She paused and pressed into a doorway as a foot patrol of the Watch passed by. Eight men with swords on their hips. Two carried whipaxes on their shoulders, the shafts two spans long. Made from ello wood, the staves bent when the axes were swung. Guards who wielded them—called whippers—studied for years to master the weapon. Like a man with a whip, whippers pulled back at the last moment of a blow, the momentum and spring force in the shaft carrying the curved axe blade toward flesh. Kila had never seen one used on a living being, but veterans spoke in hushed voice of the carnage skilled whippers left in their wakes.

The Watch passed, and their bootsteps faded to quiet. Kila continued onward, fearing for her brother, fearing for Huff, fearing what the Voluptuary would do once Wen was in her grasp.

She emerged from the narrow stairwell, legs trembling, breath heaving. Despite the chill of the slush and wintery wind coming down from the mountains, her forehead bore a sheen of sweat. No time to rest. She glanced down the Street of the Diadem. That patrol would eventually round the switchback and come this way.

Putting on all the speed she could muster, she half-ran, half-shuffled up slope. She could feel the Divide looming to her left, though none of it was visible now that the snow had increased. The Starside wall was indicated only by the occasional whale-oil lamp along its top. She doubted a patrol would be walking its parapets in this weather.

The bell tower of Ori resolved from the gloom, a great pinnacle of shadow against the darkness. She had another few staircases to climb.

She cut across the thoroughfare and to another steep stairway. Pausing momentarily to catch her breath, she checked behind her. The patrol had not appeared yet. The rattle of carriage wheels over cobblestone came from the street above. Low squawks of atlen draft birds echoed from nearby buildings.

By the time she'd made it to the top of the stairs, the carriage sounds had stopped. She needed to put her brother down, but she worried she wouldn't be able to get him back onto her shoulder. Already she'd climbed two hundred steps, and her legs didn't have much left in them. She peeked into the street.

A sleek carriage, shiny and black and emblazoned with a Radiant's crest, stood in the middle of the street. She couldn't make out the crest, but she didn't need to. She had seen this carriage and these exact blue atlens very recently. In fact, she had cut the harnesses of the atlens to create a distraction in the street so she could free the cats from two sailors.

The driver sat outboard, huddled beneath a thick cloak, hood pulled over his head. Soft light glowed through white curtains covering the door window. A stopped carriage would not have given Kila pause in any other circumstance. But there were no people on the streets, no other carriages. And atlens were not surefooted in slush.

Kila didn't see what choice she had. She couldn't stand there forever. And Wen's wheezes had become more labored. She trudged across the street, giving the carriage a wide berth. She went behind it, hoping the driver and occupants wouldn't notice her.

A clunk sounded behind her. A female voice, sharp with a Gristensider's perfect enunciation, called out: "Lass! Come here!"

Kila kept walking.

"This is no weather to be out and about in."

Kila increased her pace, hoping to make it to the next stairwell. At least there it would be too narrow for more than two people to come at her at once.

"By Kil's throbbing member, I'm not going to hurt you!"

The blasphemy stopped Kila. She turned and found a dark-haired young woman of no more than eighteen standing next to the carriage. She wore jhodpurs and a form-fitting vest beneath a dark cloak. "Please. My carriage is warm and dry."

"I need to get him to the Baths. He's very ill."

"A long walk carrying him, a short ride in my carriage."

Kila's weariness and worry battled with her suspicion. "How do you know who I am?"

"The Voluptuary sensed you needed help."

Kila wasn't convinced. Wen coughed and choked. Kila's shoulder screamed, reminding her of a recent injury. As it was, she would never be able to carry Wen the whole way. She'd have to leave him and race to the Baths in hopes that a Sensual would send novitiates back with Kila to fetch him.

She decided to risk accepting the young woman's help. She still had Cayne, after all. Stumbling toward the carriage, Kila had never felt more helpless and useless.

The woman's brows were knitted with concern, and she held a hand toward the door. "Hagle! Climb down and help this poor girl get her brother inside."

The carriage wobbled as the driver scurried down. He was short and lean, but strong. He took Wen's weight and backed into the carriage. Kila followed him in. There was a forward-facing and rear-facing bench. Hagle leaned Wen onto the front bench and slipped back into the cold. The woman climbed in and shut the door. She removed her cloak and threw it over Wen.

The driver whistled, and the atlens started to pull the carriage.

Kila sat on the edge of the bench as the woman took the opposite seat. She had wavy black hair and thin, high brows. Her large eyes glimmered, dark and alert in a lovely round face. She was plump compared to a Cheapsgater, but fit. She wore a dagger on her belt. "I'm Quinn Peline. You are Kila Sigh, correct?"

Kila nodded, suspicion rising again. Her hand went to Cayne and rested on the pommel.

"You needn't stab me, lass." Quinn leaned back and eyed the blade. "Is that blood on the hilt?"

Kila glanced down, the memory of killing the acolyte slamming her as hard as a blow to the face.

"It's . . . blood. Yes."

She had never stabbed a man before, much less killed one. She had a sudden urge to scrub the blade clean, and then scrub herself from head to toe. The acolyte had attacked her, and Wen had been convulsing, and it had happened faster than thought itself. But still . . .

Quinn Peline leaned forward and placed a hand on Kila's knee. The concern was still heavy on her brow. Kila jerked away. She didn't know this person from Kil.

Quinn frowned. "The Voluptuary must consider you and your brother quite important to dispatch me to fetch you."

"How exactly does one dispatch a Radiant to fetch a couple Cheapsgate waifs?"

"The Voluptuary is convincing. But I am not a Radiant. My mother is the Radiant."

"So you're a princess?"

"No. Only Her Enlightened's daughter would be a princess, if she had one. I am merely Lady Peline. You may call me Quinn." She turned her eyes to Wen. "What ails him?"

"A lingering cough. The chill air makes it worse."

"Why, then, would he be out in weather like this? And why in Gristenside?" Now the woman was inspecting Kila's clothes and bare feet. The Watch enforced a peculiar law in Gristenside, forbidding anyone to go about barefoot. The purpose was to discourage thieves, who found shoes noisy when sneaking. But in truth, it merely kept Cheapsgaters like Kila and her brother out of the rich quarter. The rich always found the poor unsightly.

"I tried to discourage him," Kila said. "But Wen is older—and a man—and so he is always explaining things to me as if I'm four."

Quinn did not press for more. She merely smiled at Kila's evasion. The carriage swayed as it turned a sharp corner, the final switchback before arriving at the Baths. "Where does the heat in this carriage come from?" Kila asked, looking for a small stove but finding none.

"Our tithes to Til pay for mercus heat and light." She nodded at one of two mercus light sconces on the walls. Kila held her hand close to one, felt the warmth coming off it. Envy soured her mind as she thought of how nice such a lamp would be in their Warren den. If she knew how to power one, maybe they'd have light and heat without the stink of their fish-oil lantern.

"Where did you get that lovely ring?" Quinn asked. She was looking at Kila's queller. "Is that tortoise shell?"

"It was my mother's," Kila lied. "I don't know what it's made of."

"From your tone, I gather your mother is dead."

"Yes." There was nothing more to be said on that topic, especially to a stranger. "Is it much farther?"

In answer, the carriage turned. The sound of its

wheels changed as the pavement switched from cobblestone to something smoother. And then it stopped altogether.

The carriage wobbled as the driver climbed down. He opened the door, and Kila saw the steps leading to the entry of the public baths.

As the driver helped her carry Wen down, Kila was conscious of Quinn watching her. The young woman didn't get out, didn't come with Kila as she and the driver carried Wen up the steps. They went in, and Kila was engulfed by warmth. The Sensual on duty gasped and leapt up from her desk.

They lay Wen on the floor. The driver backed up a few steps and brushed his hands together. Knuckling his brow, he nodded. "I'll be off, then."

"Get him to a bed," a voice boomed from the Dome of the Gentle Goddess. It was the Voluptuary. She strode across the hall, her steps echoing. The glimmering pools filled the air with moisture and the scent of lavender. Kila was suddenly exhausted. She felt for Nax. The cat was working her way into the compound by way of the roofs. Kila could only assume Oly was with her.

"His cat is coming," Kila said to the Voluptuary.

The woman arched an eyebrow but didn't say anything else. She uttered soft commands as two novitiates came in to collect Wen. Kila wanted to go with him, but the Voluptuary stopped her. "He will be well. Unless you intend to stay and train, you must go."

Being sent away shocked Kila. After all, the woman had wanted to make her a novitiate. "That woman you sent. How did she find me?"

The Voluptuary gave Kila a flat stare, the expression unreadable. "Just because I allowed you to leave doesn't mean my interest in you vanished."

So, the Voluptuary had been watching her. Somehow. Perhaps Yiqa had been shadowing them all this time. But if that were so, why hadn't the Alnassi woman come to their aid in the plaza?

No, Yiqa hadn't been lurking about in the slushy night. The Voluptuary wouldn't waste Yiqa's skills like that. Nor did Kila believe Yiqa would tolerate such an assignment. The Voluptuary certainly had other spies. That made sense. She was the head of a powerful Way and must have many agents under her command.

Except, Kila hadn't seen anyone following them. And with Wen, Fallo, and their cats along, Kila doubted any human could avoid their notice for long.

The Voluptuary approached Kila, arm extended toward the door. She motioned for Kila to leave. "Lady Peline may be out there still."

"I already thanked her."

"Perhaps she may be of more service to you than just delivering you and your brother here."

Kila didn't know what the woman was getting at. She decided not to ask. Her presence was not wanted. "Should I fetch Finta Sahng?"

"Finta is staying here for now. The Hargothe wanted her. And that means he must not have her."

"The Hargothe wants me, too."

"The difference is that Finta chose to stay. You see, despite her many bad choices in life, my sister is not a complete fool."

The Voluptuary practically shoved Kila out the door.

Come to me, Kila sent to Nax.

What about Wen?

Oly will find him. But you and I aren't welcome here. It wasn't completely true, but Kila doubted Nax would appreciate the nuances of her relationship with the Voluptuary.

The carriage was still there, a warm glow seeping through the curtains. Hagle sat huddled atop the vehicle, his hands gripping the atlen reins. The birds stood on one foot, their heads bowed.

The Voluptuary had been cryptic when mentioning Quinn might be waiting. She was leaving a decision up to Kila. But Kila didn't know what it was. She went to the carriage. Quinn was inside, hands folded on her lap. She brightened at the sight of Kila. "Come in, please."

Kila didn't move. "Why?"

Nax brushed against her leg. With a thought, Kila urged the cat to hide under the carriage. The Voluptuary may trust this woman, but Kila didn't.

"I live close by. I'll give you a bed for the night. You can be near to your brother."

The idea of staying at a Radiant's home was so absurd Kila couldn't help but laugh. She had assumed the only chance she would ever have of entering such a place would be to break in and rob it. And here she was, getting an invitation.

Kila spread her arms apart, showing off her soaked garments. "You do know I'm just a Cheapsgate waif, don't you? Not really trained in mansion manners." And she couldn't forget the blood on Cayne.

Lady Quinn Peline leaned forward, eyes intent. "I know the Voluptuary thought you were important enough to rouse me and my driver to fetch you. She has never called upon me to perform such a favor before. But I know her. Her request was no whim. Now, please get in. You're letting all the heat out. And poor Hagle surely wants to get to his bed."

"Has the Voluptuary told you about my, uh, little friend?"

A slight smile curved the woman's lips. "Is it with you? I would love to see it."

"Her name is Nax. And if any harm comes to her, I will burn your house down with you in it."

The smile disappeared. The woman became very grave. "Understood."

Kila knew the driver couldn't see Nax from where he was seated, so she sent to the cat, *Climb in. It's safe. I think.*

Nax didn't need much encouragement. She was cold and wet. Like a gray ghost, she glided into the carriage. Quinn gasped at the sight of her. Nax jumped onto the bench opposite the woman. Kila closed the door behind herself and joined her cat, who immediately climbed onto her lap to steal Kila's warmth.

"I've read about cats," Quinn said, voice full of wonder. "I never thought I would see one." She extended a hand, tentatively. "May I?"

"You'd better let me ask her first."

Quinn's eyes widened, and her mouth opened. "What?"

May this woman touch you? Kila sent.

Nax didn't answer so much as stretch and roll onto her back. This was an invitation to have her belly scratched. Kila nodded to Quinn.

The woman stroked Nax's belly, mouth open in awe. "She's so soft."

"That's enough of that." Kila didn't want the woman to assume too much familiarity with Nax. And it was always good to withhold something from someone. That gave you power. How much, Kila didn't know. But she was dealing with a lady of a major house. She needed all the leverage she could get.

The carriage started forward again. Quinn continued to watch Nax in fascination. Kila wondered how the Voluptuary had gained such influence over the woman. Perhaps Quinn had been a novitiate. Maybe she had some small spark of the mercus. That was probably it. The woman had trained at the Baths, then returned home to resume her life of luxury. She had probably grown fond of the Voluptuary during her time there, felt she owed the woman.

"Are you hungry?" Quinn asked.

"I'm from Cheapsgate. I'm always hungry."

Quinn laughed, shaking her head as if Kila was the most marvelous thing she had ever seen. "I think we shall test the limits of your appetite."

The carriage pulled to a stop. Quinn nodded for Kila to climb down. Holding Nax in her arms, she exited the carriage and found herself standing at the rear of one of the great houses of Gristenside. The manse stretched a hundred paces in either direction. Tidy brickwork, manicured lawns, windows shining with mercus lights. The house was larger than any Terriside inn.

"Welcome to our city house," Quinn said. The way she said it suggested there were many other homes belonging to the Family Peline. Such wealth was beyond the ken of a girl of Kila's experience. Already her thief's mind was considering possibilities. She would never steal from someone offering hospitality. But there was much to be learned inside such a house.

They entered through a back door, and Kila stepped into a new world.

9

NO ONE ELSE

Kila was familiar with anger, joy, and hatred. But she had never experienced guilt until snuggling into the soft bed Lady Quinn Peline provided for her. The young woman said it had belonged to a maid who had recently left her service. Kila could not believe that a mere maid could have such a gloriously luxurious existence.

Her stomach bulged from the feast she'd enjoyed. Her skin was warm, soft, and clean. She wore a soft nightgown and was covered with a thick down-stuffed comforter. Nax was nestled underneath it, already asleep.

Kila knew Wen was resting comfortably, because Oly and Nax had been talking. Finta had administered more of her medicines to ease his breathing.

But it was Fallo and Henley that Kila was thinking of as guilt crept into her innards. Lop was too far away for Nax to communicate with. Nax believed Fallo and his cat were still sneaking around Terriside and leading Donse Masters in circles. For all his fantasizing about luxury, he had proved his loyalty by enduring extreme discomfort to aid his friends. Kila sighed discontentedly as she snuggled into her warm bed. And poor Henley . . .

There was nothing she could do for either of them tonight. Exhaustion made her head feel stuffed full of wool.

Her eyes drifted to a mahogany bureau across the room. She had placed Cayne there after washing the blade and hilt. An odd thing, though. There hadn't been any blood on the blade itself, just on the hilt. Kila shivered, recalling the image of the acolyte's wide-eyed look of shock as death claimed him.

She snuggled more deeply into the bed and closed her eyes. She tried to ignore the ache in her throat. Why should she care about an acolyte of Til? The man had been there when Henley had suffered such agony, and he'd been holding Wen down. And he had attacked her.

And yet she knew she had made the man's heart stop and his life's blood drain from his body. She had done it. No one else. She had.

With all these alien and painful feelings roiling in her heart, Kila slipped into nightmares.

10

THE CRUELTY OF HOPE

Time passes in fits and starts when one is locked in darkness. Henley did not know if he'd been in the Abbey cell for a few days or a few weeks. There was no light except when an acolyte slipped a bowl of gruel through the door. The stink of his own excretions was the only constant. And though the man claiming to be Dunne Yples in the cell next door regularly erupted into frenzies of screams and ravings, one could not judge time by the cries and silences of a madman.

Henley's own fits of panic followed no schedule either. His fists and feet were bruised and sore, his nails crusted with dried blood from his attempts to kick and claw his way out. Exhaustion was Henley's ally now, for in it he felt nothing at all. He imagined this was how a caged animal felt after a while. Numb and hopeless.

He wished for the numbness to grow, to blot out all his senses, even his thoughts. There would be no escape. There would be no future. Might as well join the rest of his family in oblivion. Had he the energy—and the slightest clue how to accomplish it—he would have taken his own life right then.

As it was, he slept. And when he wasn't asleep, he lay on his back and stared into nothingness, carried upon swirls of color produced by his own madness. Sometimes it was even peaceful. Perhaps he would soon join Dunne Yples in his raves.

In this state, he doubted everything his senses reported to him. Was the light seeping beneath his cell door truly there, or merely a figment of his derangement? Was the smell of baking bread a fantasy, or a true waft of goodness passing by on a tray borne by an acolyte?

So when a voice spoke to him inside his head, he did not immediately respond.

Henley? it said again. *Do you hear me?*

Henley sat upright, smacking his head on the low, angled ceiling of his cell. He pressed a filthy palm to his forehead and moaned.

Are you there? I feel you.

I'm here, Huff, he sent to his beloved cat. *I'm locked in the Abbey.*

I'm here, too.

A sob tore from Henley's throat. This was worse than being trapped. Now his cat had been caught. A feeling of fear passed through the bond, making Henley hunch forward. The sensation had no concept to it, but Henley recognized what it meant. Huff was hiding.

You haven't been caught!

Not yet.

Don't let them catch you. Get out of there.

No response except irritation. Cats did not like being told obvious things. Henley rammed his shoulder against the door. "Let me out, you Kil-kissing sons of—of—morons!"

Dunne Yples shrieked. "Dem-Kisk! Dem-Kisk!"

Henley regretted his own cries. Now he'd awakened the lunatic in the next cell. If history was any guide, the man would now shout and scream for the next eternity or two.

Where are you? Huff sent.

In a cell. It has to be a dungeon beneath the Abbey. Where are you?

Big room. Many robe-men hunt me.

Henley had been in the Cathedral many times, before the Keels had burned his house down and killed his father. *Let me see.*

He sensed a moment of resistance, but then his vision shifted. The sudden change made him dizzy. He lay on his back and tried to breathe deeply. The catsight always made him throw up.

Through Huff's eyes he saw the floor of a side chapel. The light was very dim. Sounds reached his ears, reverberant and confused. Huff's hearing. The spicy smell of incense hit his nose. With the connection to Huff intensified, Henley's body tensed and he hunkered into himself. His heart sped up in sympathy with Huff's.

He tried to pass along a calming feeling. It didn't do much good. Huff's ears were alert to every noise, his body coiled and ready to spring. Henley decided that was a good thing.

What are you hiding behind? he asked. A dark column stood right in the middle of his vision, but he couldn't focus on it. Huff remained in control of where he looked. When Henley turned his head, the vision did not follow. The effect made his stomach lurch.

I don't know. A thing.

Can you get up high? There's a pulpit at the side of the nave.

A what?

It's a raised platform where the Donse Masters deliver their sermons. Like a little balcony with stairs leading up to it.

I saw that.

Can you sneak up to it?

No.

Henley had to interpret that no. It didn't mean the cat couldn't climb stairs; it meant the cat wasn't willing to leave his hiding spot. That was fine. *Stay hidden. When you think it's safe, stay hidden longer. The*

Donse Masters will lay traps. Don't approach any food. It will be a trap.

I understand.

Once you get up high where you can see the whole room, let me see. I can show you the door they took me through.

Good. I'll tell Lop.

How did you get in?

Wen brought me so I could sneak around.

That was a relief. At least Huff hadn't been captured by someone seeking to collect the bounty. And with Wen involved, it suggested there was a plan.

The cruelty of hope. Henley's spirits collapsed. Even knowing which door he'd been dragged through would do Wen and the others no good. They'd have to pass dozens of Donse Masters and acolytes and come into an area forbidden to anyone not of the Way.

You should try to get out, he sent to Huff. *Get away.*

You should try to get out. Get away, Huff responded.

Henley laughed despite his tears. Huff had experimented with humor a few times before, but this was the first time he'd made Henley laugh—and he'd made a good point at the same time. Huff was right. If the situation were reversed, Henley knew he would risk his own life to save Huff's. No question.

If either of them were going to get out, they both were. So they might as well work together. Huff stopped sending the catsight, and darkness returned to Henley's vision. He reviewed what he knew about his cell. He'd seen the hallway outside the two times he'd been led to the eyeless old man's chamber.

He started envisioning it. Every door, every wall sconce, every turn. The stairs leading down. The smell of wet stone. The tomb markers. The quietude. He remembered the acolytes, silent and strong. Nothing he recalled sparked an idea of how to escape.

Now he hoped he'd be summoned to the old man again soon. There was too much he hadn't bothered to notice. But one thing stood out: There were no guards patrolling the hallways. They didn't need them because the cell doors were so secure. What did the locks look like? Henley couldn't remember. Were there locks at all? Or perhaps just latches on the outside.

Kila took Wen to get help, Huff sent. *He coughs blood.*

And where is Fallo?

Lurking. Sneaking. Hiding.

Good. You do the same.

Always.

11

———

A HISS FOR KILA

The raven stands atop a tombstone amid a dreary cemetery. *Sleep, Kila Sigh. Sleep.*

A shadow passes over the bird, cast by a young woman. She is slight, strong. Her gown is velvet, thickly lined against the cold. Ermine fur trims the sleeves and lines her hood, a sure sign of great wealth. She carries a small embroidered pouch cinched shut with a golden cord, the tassels of which drape over her pale hand. She opens the pouch and pulls out a wedge of bread. She tears off a small piece and extends her hand toward the raven.

With slow steps, she approaches. The bird's head cocks to the side, black eyes watching her. It is not afraid.

Sleep, Kila Sigh! Sleep!

The raven snatches the bread from the young woman's fingers.

The woman speaks. "I'm waiting. Come to me." She lowers her hood. Black hair, some loose, some worked in intricate braids, falls over her shoulders. Her eyes pierce the soul.

The raven flutters, then flies away.

Sleep! Sleep! Sleep! SLEEP!

A WASH of pure terror awakened Kila. She sat up in the soft bed, heart slamming in her chest. Her hair stuck to her sweat-slicked forehead. Nax stood next to her, back arched, fur standing up.

What is it? Kila sent.

Surging fear came from the cat. Kila looked all around, but in the dim of her chamber she spotted no threat. She put her hands on the cat and received a hiss and swat in return. No claws, fortunately.

"Nax! What is it?" Her voice broke through the cat's fear. Nax calmed enough to stop hissing. The wave of terror receded from Kila's body, allowing her to relax somewhat. She discovered her hands had been tensed into claws.

It's Oly, Nax sent. *Something is very wrong.*

Kila was out of bed and out of her nightgown in seconds. Her garments had been laid out to dry when she'd gone to bed. They were still a bit damp, but she pulled them on anyway, ignoring the chill against her skin.

Lady Quinn Peline had sent in a pair of boots for

Kila to try on, but she'd gone straight to bed before bothering. She ignored them now and left the room. Nax trotted after her. They went out the rear door, then along a short gravel drive to the Street of the Diadem.

The gates were open, the guard asleep in his shack. It was dark, but the sky to the east was hazy with the first hints of dawn. Enough light crept over the city that Kila could make out the bell tower above the Baths of Ori. Kila sprinted toward it, feet sloshing through the icy slush covering the street.

When she arrived at the public baths, she found the Sensual on duty gathering her items and preparing to go off to bed. The replacement Sensual was taking a seat. When Kila barged in, cat in tow, both turned and gaped.

"Where's my brother?" Kila said, breathless.

Kila recognized the woman being relieved. Sens Beth. She had been at this post when Kila had brought Wen. The new Sensual was one of the Iopsi ladies. Dark-skinned, lovely, but frowning in disapproval.

Sens Beth pointed vaguely across the circular hall of the baths. "I believe the Voluptuary had him taken to the novitiates' ward."

"Take me there. Now."

"Miss Sigh, you do recall I was here when the Voluptuary made you to leave, don't you?"

"Wen is in trouble. Something's happening to him. Right now."

Oly is panicking, Nax sent.

Kila pointed at Nax. "She's telling me Wen is in trouble. She's talking to Wen's cat right now."

The Iopsi woman made a strange motion with her hand. It looked like a ward against evil.

Sens Beth let a worried look come over her brow. She twisted her lips and tapped her pinched fingers together. All at once, she gave in. "Follow me."

"But Sens Beth," said the Iopsi woman, "she shouldn't be allowed in the novitiates' ward unless she's committing to her training."

Kila arched an eyebrow at Sens Beth. "Lead me or I'll go in through the gardens. The wall of my old room was turned to dust recently. Left a hole as good as a door. Remember?"

"The animals can speak to each other, Sens Taht," Sens Beth said the Iopsi woman. "I trust that much. There is no harm in checking, and much harm if she tells the truth and we do nothing."

Sens Taht glowered at Kila but said nothing else.

Kila urged Sens Beth to lead the way. The woman refused to run, but she did walk quickly. She was Kila's height but at least a ten-year older. She wore her hair in a no-nonsense trim, which might have made her look boyish if her tremendous bosom hadn't been such a force to be reckoned with.

Impatience ate at Kila as they wound out of the baths and through a maze of corridors. Nax wasn't responding to her inquiries anymore. All she received from the little gray was tension and worry.

The Sensual finally increased her pace when screams erupted ahead. The first body they encountered was a novitiate. A girl of indeterminate age because her head was missing. They found it further down the hall. She couldn't have been more than fourteen. Her lips were pulled back in a grimace of terror and pain.

Sens Beth swayed suddenly. Kila realized the woman was about to faint. She helped the Sensual sit and lean against the wall. A boy of ten was standing nearby, staring. Kila snapped her fingers at him. "Throw a sheet over the girl's face and then fetch water for Sens Beth."

She didn't wait to see if her orders were obeyed before racing down the corridor.

Where is Oly? she sent to Nax. *Show me the way.* Nax darted ahead and slipped down a stairwell. Kila realized the cat was taking her to the level where her own room had been. A new worry blossomed in her chest. Ragin was down there.

The second body she encountered was intact, but there was no life in it. She recognized the gray beard and the stained robes. Sens Goolsoy. Kila didn't want to look. Despite her mistrust of the Sensuals, she had liked Goolsoy. He had been so eager to train her, to help her tap the full potential of her powers. Now that would never happen.

She didn't spare him more than a glance, her mind intent on finding her brother.

A sickening certainty crept into her mind. She knew who had done this. *What* had done this. The demayne. No human could have killed that novitiate so viciously. And perhaps Goolsoy's mercus powers had protected him from decapitation. Maybe his efforts had left him open to some other sort of attack. The demayne's power was greater than Goolsoy's. Greater than anyone's.

She passed the door to her own room. No one would be sleeping in there with the wall disintegrated. Two novitiates stood at a doorway further down, staring into the room beyond. One, a girl with thick blond hair, pressed a hand to her mouth. The other was Ragin. He leaned away from the door, his arms up as if to ward off an impending attack. Their faces were ghastly, lit by a familiar greenish hue. A roiling fog spilled from the doorway and curled around their shins.

Kila shoved them aside. *Stay back,* she sent to Nax.

She crossed the threshold. The demayne stood in the middle of the room, arms crossed. A green glow swirled all around him. His heavy brow conveyed disdain more than anger or hatred. Pinned against the rear wall, feet above the floor, arms splayed, was Wen. His head lolled, his lips were slack.

Kila couldn't see Oly, which meant Wen's cat was

somewhere under the green fog. "Release him," she demanded.

The demayne turned, seeming to notice Wen for the first time. Instead of speaking into her mind, it opened its mouth and said, "You mean the boy? Why would you care about him?"

She realized she had drawn Cayne at some point. She stood in the fighter's crouch Yiqa had taught her. "Let him down. The Voluptuary is coming."

The demayne did not seem concerned. That worried Kila, because the Voluptuary had borne the weird glowing orb that had chased the demayne away when he'd first come for Kila. The demayne walked toward Wen, considered him a moment, then grasped him by the throat. The demayne spoke to Kila over his shoulder, "You saw my handiwork in the corridor. You know I can tear his head off and drain him."

But he hadn't killed Wen yet. That meant the creature had been waiting for her to come. Whatever he'd done to Wen had been to lure her here.

Ragin was at her side now, hands balled into fists. "Get away, foul demayne!" His voice shook, but his face was set in determination.

The demayne regarded Ragin for a moment, then flicked his finger. Ragin flew backward through the door. The blond girl screamed, but the sound muted when the door slammed shut of its own accord.

The demayne smiled. "Your brother's life is in your

hands, Kila Sigh. You and your Beloved One will come with me. Hesitate, and I will kill him."

Kila remembered the *filla* needle the Voluptuary had pinned through her shirt. Her fingers found it. She wondered if it would work on a demayne. "Set him down and I'll go with you."

The demayne released Wen's neck and the boy took to the air. He floated across the room and flopped into the fog. Kila raced to his side. She found him lying on a cot. She hefted his head clear of the roiling mist. Wen's breath came in short, shallow gulps. She'd never seen him breathe so poorly. Oly jumped up next to him, sparing a hiss for Kila.

Oly says you should go with the demayne and never come back.

"Call in your Beloved One," the demayne ordered.

Kila didn't have to summon Nax. She felt the small gray pressing against her shin.

Kila gently lay Wen's head down and picked up her cat. Nax didn't tremble or recoil from the demayne. The huge creature beckoned Kila toward him with a long, clawed finger. She obeyed, this time of her own choice. The green swirl intensified and widened to encompass her, Nax, and the demayne.

"Be very still," the demayne said.

A freezing wind blew from above, chilling her to the marrow. And then her sight filled with green light and the novitiates' chamber vanished.

12

RECOVERY AGENT

Dunne Marlow had just arrived at the Derslin Wheel when the demayne Flaumishtak arrived. The green light dimmed, revealing the huge creature. The demayne dwarfed the girl, and she was made smaller by the way she hunched from the beast, her arms around a small gray cat.

"Marvelous!" Marlow said, rubbing his hands together. He hadn't seen a cat in ages. His brother, Tenn, had always been fascinated by the creatures. Had always wanted to bond with one despite the prohibition by the Way of Til. Tenn was the Hargothe now, and it appeared he would finally have a cat of some use. All the others he had collected over the years had refused to speak to him. Whether that was because they didn't like him, or they weren't infested with Beloved Ones . . . who knew?

"Your Beloved One is remarkable, Miss Sigh," Marlow said, approaching her and grinning.

The girl glanced from him to the demayne and back. "So yer the Kil-lickin' arse-cork who controls this talkin' moose. Shoulda known it'd be a Donse Master."

Her Cheaps dialect came at him so rapid and thick he needed a moment to interpret it. But once he had, he laughed. "Charming."

The demayne crossed its arms and stared down its wide, flat nose at Marlow. "I believe you owe me payment for services rendered." Its voice was gravel grinding against iron. The sound of it made the girl wince and jump back.

Flaumishtak paused a moment, eyeing the girl with utter disdain. He raised a finger. The black claw on the end gleamed. "If you were to turn her over to me, I might be willing to discuss a further engagement."

That was a demayne for you. Always wanting more, always scheming up some bargain or other. "Sorry, Flaumishtak, but this will conclude our dealings. For now, anyway." Marlow removed a pouch from his belt and held it out. The demayne plucked it up and peered inside. Satisfied, he bowed slightly and vanished in a swirl of green light.

Kila Sigh was looking all around. "Where am I?" She had set the cat down. It was nosing among the columns of the wheel. That would never do.

"Call your animal back, please. We must go."

She turned her face toward him. Had he been a younger man—much younger—he might have been instantly smitten. She was not beautiful in the usual sense. Her features were sharp, her mouth a bit wide. And yet, what marvelously striking eyes. And a brow as expressive and delicate as one might find on the face of a Radiant. She needed to put on weight. She looked just like what she was. A hungry stray.

He noticed a ring on her finger. "That explains your absence upon the mercusine," he said, nodding at her hand. "The Voluptuary was wise to keep such a relic from the Way of Til." He held out his hand. "May I see it? No, don't take it off. Just give me your hand."

She struck like a snake, black blade streaking. The point drove into his chest. Not far in, perhaps the width of a pinky, before clunking to a stop. He fell back and the tip of the blade slipped free. He pressed a hand to his chest as a sharp pain blossomed.

The girl recovered her balance and crouched, the blade held before her. Someone had been teaching her. Fortunately, Marlow had long ago learned to ward himself against such attacks. That the blade had pierced his skin at all intrigued him. It seemed Kila Sigh was full of surprises.

"A Shadline as well as a merculyn? What else might you do, speak to the small gods? Whisper to the eldritch fires?" He pulled his hand away from his wound. Wiped his thumb across the dabs of blood on his fingertips. "Perhaps you are a demayne yourself, Kila Sigh."

The girl did not move or even blink. Her cat sat ten paces behind her, tail wrapped around its feet. Its eyes flashed in the lantern light.

He dug a kerchief from his pocket and stuffed it beneath his robes to stanch the flow of blood. It took a fair amount of will not to back away from the angry girl. He feigned amusement to put her off guard.

The girl's blade was as long as her forearm, black steel. A sheath was strapped to her right leg. He sighed. Of course, Flaumishtak hadn't confiscated it. The beast was probably laughing even now at the thought of her shoving the weapon into Marlow's gut.

"Per'aps you are th' demayne," she said. "There be naught but stone beneath yer flesh."

"Alas, no. I merely ward myself against attacks such as yours. You see, I am not particularly well-liked at the moment. Many have reason to want me dead." Marlow's fingers went to his throat and he pulled forth the amulet he wore on a leather cord. A simple bit of carved wood, a depiction of a fish jumping from a pond. Unskilled hands, perhaps a child's, had done the work. And yet it was a queller like the girl's ring.

He removed it, felt the mercus thrum through him. A bit of concentration readied him. If she lunged again, she would discover the mercus could be a subtler weapon than she realized.

He glowered at the hole in his robes. "Mending

garments is beyond my powers. Perhaps you could . . . ? No? Well, it didn't hurt to ask. I shall have to find thread somewhere."

Marlow had a problem now. Namely, he was bleeding and in no small amount of pain. He needed to get back to the jewelry shop and tend to his wound, but the girl was still brandishing her blade.

"I assure you, I mean you no harm, Kila Sigh. You may sheathe your weapon."

"If you don't mean me harm, why send a demayne to fetch me?"

"Like you, I am a recovery agent of sorts," he said. "I simply return things to their rightful owners. And you, my dear, belong to the Hargothe."

"I belong to no one."

"The Hargothe *is* no one." He picked up his lantern and started walking. She didn't follow. "Unless you can create light with your mercus powers, you will find yourself lost in the dark in a matter of moments. Best to come with me." He kept walking.

Kila Sigh did not follow. No matter. She would wander away from the Derslin Wheel eventually, and there was only one exit. He would patch himself up and await her there.

13

DROP THE CHEAPS

The Donse Master disappeared into the gloom, his lantern light shrinking to a pinpoint of light. That such a vast distance could exist without a sky overhead made Kila's spine shrink into itself. There must be a ceiling, but . . . how? What could hold it up? Surely not the circle of columns. She'd seen the top caps before the Donse Master had gone. They supported nothing.

Nax returned to her as the darkness pressed in. The strange columns had long passed into darkness.

I can't feel Oly or Lop or Huff or Startle right now, Nax sent. The statement came with a sort of muted feeling, as if hearing something through layers of wool blankets.

But they're still there, right? Nax? The others are still there?

No. A pulse of anxiety came through.

Odd. Nax always knew which direction his litter-mates were in.

Where are we? Nax sent.

Kila had no idea. The demayne had moved her and Nax a great distance, she thought. But it had happened in a frozen moment. It may have taken a thousand years, or half a heartbeat. Based on her conversation with the Donse Master, she guessed it had been closer to the half a heartbeat.

I stabbed him with Cayne, but it didn't go all the way in.

Nax had no response to that. She put her paws on Kila's knee, a clear sign she was ready to be picked up. Kila obliged, happy to have her warm friend close to her.

The anxiety still seeped from Nax. But Kila had enough of her own to keep her stomach in knots. She had been abducted by a demayne and then she'd stabbed another man. And it hadn't done more than cut him when it should have killed him.

She wasn't sure which bothered her more: Her attempt to kill, or her failure.

The pinpoint of light vanished. By then the lantern was so far away it made no difference in what she could see, which was nothing. But now she felt unrooted. If not for the pressure of her own weight on her feet, she might have doubted which way was down.

The demayne had used mercus powers to bring

her here. That was obvious. But she couldn't begin to imagine what combinations of the senses would go into such a feat. And yet the Donse Master had controlled the beast, had called him Flaumishtak. The name curled across her mind.

She was reminded of the Voluptuary's warning about demayne and names. *At least he didn't call me Delicious One again.*

The demayne is dangerous, Nax said. *But I fear this place more.*

Kila couldn't disagree. The main thing was to get out of there. She could worry about the Donse Master and the demayne later.

One thing was obvious to her: The only way out of this darkness was to go in the direction the Donse Master had gone. Why else would he have left her alone here?

But that wasn't true. The demayne had left by different means. Kila urged Nax onto her shoulder and removed her queller. The mercus came alive to her.

She smelled the demayne's odor of burnt hair—what Sens Renna had called "taint-tell"—and a hint of spice, too. Maybe the Donse Master had doused himself with scent. That wasn't uncommon, for the Theb warned that bathing too often placed improper attention on the body.

Relaxing her vision, Kila searched for metal. Instantly, strange symbols emerged all around her. She recognized them immediately. They were from the columns. They glowed a brilliant white light that blurred into blue at the fringes. The nearest symbol was three slashes, slanting from left to right.

She approached, holding her hand out to feel the column lest she bump into it. The glow of metals did not cast light on anything else, so it didn't illuminate the circle.

She had never seen this color of glow before, so she didn't know what the metal could be. Rare, surely. She closed her eyes and listened. There. A high, singing tone. Not piercing, but bell-like. Pure. The air smelled earthy and damp now.

She ran a fingertip down one of the lines. It was debossed into a flat section carved into the column. The line was smooth like glass, and warm. Her mercus senses came alive. Some notion—a certainty beneath the level of thought—aligned in her awareness. Without understanding more than the idea of "brighten," she lent the three lines more glow.

The slashes flared in response. A gust of balmy air fluttered Kila's hair back. The smell of wet sand and the sound of pounding surf came next.

Up and down switched. Kila lost her balance. Nax cried out and clamped her claws into Kila's shoulder.

She fell back, the floor slamming into her back and knocking the wind from her lungs.

The symbols faded, and all that remained was the

faint smell of the ocean and the grit of sand under her fingernails.

But Kila hadn't gone anywhere. The darkness still engulfed her and the floor was just the same. Whatever she had done, it had not vanished her the way the demayne had done.

She picked herself off the floor and turned all around, trying to sense which way the Donse Master had gone. She wanted nothing more than to leave this place. Even if she had to face the Hargothe.

She managed to recall the glow of the symbols, though they showed very faintly now. The three slashes were now across the circle from her. She must have flown back much farther than she'd thought. Now the nearest symbol was a triangle with a circle inside.

She thought the Donse Master had walked away from the slashes, so she skirted the triangle and plunged into the emptiness beyond. Nax rode on her shoulder, tail curling around Kila's neck.

The sharp edges of the queller pressed into Kila's palm. In the absolute darkness of this place, her mercus senses were all that allowed her to keep her balance.

Though she couldn't see ahead, she could feel ahead. She discovered it helped to keep her eyes closed, allowing the level of the floor, the texture of the stone, and the vague solidity of the air create a mental image of what lay before her. She extended her awareness up and up. No ceiling. At least, none within the range of her mercus senses.

The door emerged in her mind long before she came to it. And when she finally reached it, she knew to stop. She reached out, grasped the handle she knew was there, and swung the door open on silent hinges.

She stepped through and found herself in a dimly-lit tunnel. At the end of it, a stone wall blocked the way. And yet . . . her mercus senses felt through it to a space beyond.

She stepped into the wall. Through the wall. A wash of cold sent chills up her arms and legs.

"Best put that queller back on, love," said the Donse Master. He was sitting on a barrel, hands folded on his lap. His lantern burned brightly next to him, but now it illuminated his whole face. He was stocky, with salt-and-pepper hair and beard. He might have been handsome once but had gone soft in his middle years. He offered his usual mocking smile. "The Hargothe is certainly not the only one seeking you now."

"So yer givin' me t' the Hargothe," she said. "Fer yer sake, I hope he pays well."

The man smiled and absently scratched his chin. "You have no idea."

Kila felt the shape of the cellar. A stairwell lay on the other side. If she could get there before him, she might be able to escape. He did not look particularly fit.

"Put the ring back on," he said again. "I prefer to be amiable, but if required I can become quite forceful."

Kila obeyed and slipped the ring on. The loss of her mercus senses sent a keen feeling of disappointment through her. Her walk in darkness had showed her so much about the power. She wanted to use it more, explore the world with it, feeling as if she'd truly opened her eyes for the first time. "Ya sure have a prissy way o' talkin' fer a forceful man."

"Drop the Cheaps-talk, girl. I can't understand such ignorance."

"That's its own sort o' ignerince, innit?"

Instead of rising to the bait, he smiled. "I suppose it is. But please, let us be civil to each other. It will go easier for you the more compliant you learn to be."

"Then it won't go easy for me."

She ran for it, sending her intentions to Nax at the same time. She darted past the astonished Donse Master while Nax leapt over barrels and crates.

14

IT CAME UP SKULLS

Kila found the stairwell and pounded up the rickety steps. Shoulder down, she barged through the door at the top and into a kitchen.

Five large men stood there, arms crossed and looking bored. They straightened at once and moved to block the exits.

"Don't harm her!" the Donse Master called from below. He came in behind Kila. He nodded to a stocky, bald man with thick fingers. "Not too much, anyway. I'll meet you there."

The Donse Master wove through the men and left the kitchen. The men closed in, the head goon's face coldly determined.

Nax, go! she sent.

The cat tried to slip through one man's legs, but was instantly snared in a net.

Two men grabbed Kila by the arms, their hands gripping her like iron shackles.

"Ya don't hafta pop my arms off. I'm not resistin', my friend," she said.

"I'm not yer friend. Hood her!"

A musty sailcloth bag went over her head. Someone bound her hands, cinching her wrists behind her so tightly her skin burned under the rope.

"No, leave the ring," the boss warned. "Marlow will notice if you take it. And then it'll be my neck."

Someone mumbled a curse, then Kila was shoved forward. Once outside they threw her onto a hard wooden surface. It started moving. A wagon.

Nax, what do you see?

In answer, Nax sent Kila the catsight. The sudden shift in perspective made Kila's stomach lurch. The weaves of a net blocked much of her vision, but she saw the men sitting on the back of a wagon. And she saw herself just an arm's length away, lying face down, cheek pressed to the oily planks of the wagon bed.

The sense of being pinned made her shrug her shoulders. They moved freely. It was Nax who couldn't move. The net had been wrapped so tightly, the cat was paralyzed.

That's enough, she sent. Her vision went black as the inside of the sailcloth sack returned. The binding dug into her wrists, but at least her fingers were free. Not that she could feel them. Her hands tingled as the rope numbed all sensation except the agony of a million pinpricks.

"That's a fine lookin' blade," one man said.

"Leave it," said the boss.

"Where d'ya think she got it?"

"Stole it."

"Let's take a look at it."

"I said leave it!" A dull thump followed.

A man groaned in response. "What does a Donse Master need with a blade?"

"That isn't yer concern. Now clamp yer lips or I'll stuff a fish betwixt 'em."

Grumbling.

Fallo is coming, Nax sent.

Kila wished she knew where she was. She hadn't seen any of their surroundings in Nax's vision. If she could get the ring off, maybe she could use her mercus sense to figure it out. But the way her hands were bound, the backs of her hands were pressed together. Her fingers weren't nimble enough to get the ring off.

"Watch patrol," someone called from the front.

"Throw yon tarpaulin over her."

The weight of a heavy sheet fell over her, muffling the clatter of the wagon rolling over cobblestone.

How far is Fallo? she sent.

Nax had no idea of distance. The boy didn't stand a chance against so many men anyway. She considered her predicament and realized she knew where they were taking her. If the Hargothe wanted her, that meant the Abbey.

Tell Fallo we're being taken to the Abbey. He should go to the Baths and ask to speak to the Voluptuary and tell her that I'm in trouble.

I've told Lop.

And?

Lop says that Fallo wants to know what else is new.

This is not the time for jokes, Kila sent.

Who's joking?

Kila gave up. Despite a penchant for inappropriate humor, Fallo could be relied on to do the right thing. She hoped. The question was whether the Sensual on duty at the Baths would obstruct Fallo or help him.

Kila rolled onto her side. Nobody stopped her, so she worked her way onto her knees.

"That's far enough," the leader of the group said. "Dunne Marlow won't pay us if you fall off and get broken."

Marlow. So that's who the Donse Master was. Kila recognized the name. Something about a scandal. "Didn't he have dalliance with a Spinster?"

She didn't give a rat's whisker about Dunne Marlow's bed secrets. She just wanted her guard to keep talking.

She shifted back until her hands touched the side rail of the wagon bed. Good. Nobody behind her. She shifted her legs out from under her and leaned against the rail. Pushing her shoulders back helped ease tension in her bindings. Not enough to get free, but enough to get a thumb under the edge of the queller ring.

"He doesn't want us talkin' about that," the guard said. "Doesn't want you talkin' at all."

"Suits me fine," she said. "But just outta perfess'nal curiosity, what does kidnappin' a Cheapsgate raga-muffin pay these days?"

He laughed. The other men snickered.

She eased the ring over the knuckle, got it between two fingers, and slipped it off. She couldn't make a tight fist, but she could curl her fingers enough to keep hold on the ring.

The zing came over her. The sound of the wheels joined the creak of the axle and the scratch of atlen talon on the street. The smell of sweaty men, baking bread, and chimney smoke filled her nose. Voices of pedestrians wafted to her ears, accented with the clipped syllables typical of Terriside merchants, educated but informal. Like Fallo and Henley.

The weight of the tarp was pulling her head forward. She desperately wanted to get the hood off and breathe fresh air. The feeling of suffocation made concentrating difficult, but she relaxed into her mercus vision.

The glow of metals popped into view. Nails holding down the planks of the wagon, iron axle, blades at the belts of the men guarding her. This wasn't the place to do the iron in the blood trick, even if she had the slightest clue how to begin.

Mercus lamp posts went by. The zing helped her calm a bit, made her feel slightly less blind to her environment. She turned her attention forward, to the wagon driver. He had some copper plugs in a purse, no weapon.

"Where is Dunne Marlow?" she asked.

Silence.

The man closest to her had a brass belt buckle and a stubby knife on his belt. He, too, had a pouch of coin. She studied the glow. "I bet those skillets are burnin' a hole in yer purse. Yer prolly thinkin' 'bout all the trezz yer gonna slurp down just as soon as ya turn me over to whoever yer turnin' me over to. Did you tell yer men you already have . . . let me see . . . a couple dozen gold skillets?"

A sharp blow caught her ankle. "Shut up."

Though she couldn't see them, she sensed the other men had gone very still.

"That's prolly just the advance payment, innit? Let me guess, half up front an' half when I'm delivered. What'd ya tell yer men? Fifteen gold skillets total? Smart. You can divvy up fifteen among the five of you —three for you—and you also pocket the other half when Marlow plops the rest in yer greedy paws. I have ta say, I didn't guess you to be so devious."

Another blow. Kila hissed and bent her knees to pull her feet away from him.

"The girl's lying. How could she know what the payment is?"

Kila continued, "I know what the rest o' these men have . . . Well, that one with the silver chain 'round his neck has four silver plugs. The one with the dirk hidden in his right boot has three copper plugs and a silver skillet. The other two don't have so much as a lint ball between 'em. A pity it is, that two Til-fearin' men have nothin', while their boss is totin' a purse so heavy it makes him lean ta one side."

A flash of white glow warned Kila to duck. The boss had a silver ring on his hand and it came toward her. The blow grazed the side of her head, snagging her hood. Unfortunately, it didn't pull the Kil-damned thing off.

"How does she know what we have?" a man said. "How?"

"Forget how," said another man. "I wanna know why Grig is holding back our pay."

"Easy to figure that," Kila said. "Grig's a greedy drunkard and wants it all fer himself. Just as you've been suspectin' fer a long time."

"That's true. Grig, I think you should pay us now."

"Is what Marlow told me true, Grig?" Kila said. "That you an' him agreed that the fewer men left standin' in the end, the more money for ya both? If the Highest truly wants me, then fifteen or even fifty gold skillets is nothin'. Ten times that is more like it. By Kil's blazin' brow, I think I'd turn *muhself* in fer five hundred skillets! Five hundred, men. And Grig is keepin' it all fer himself!"

"Five hundred?" said one of the underlings. "Now look here, Grig. I know you get a bigger cut for bossin' this crew, but you told me I'd get three skillets. That don't sound fair if you get five hundred."

"At *least* five hundred," Kila said. "Tilsday collection at the Cathedral brings in three thousand, I heard once."

"She's right about that. I heard that, too."

"Stifle yer yappers!" Grig shrieked. "Just you stifle yer Kil-kissing lips, all of you. Yer a bunch of slag-brained sons of Sourwater carp!" Grig had moved forward, hand on his stubby knife hilt, gauging by the position of his silver ring.

Kila rolled toward the rear of the wagon, searching for a tailgate. There was none. She could roll right off the back. Problem was, she couldn't leave Nax behind.

The wagon turned sharply and then came to a stop. Grig was shouting at the men not to trust the captive and how stupid were they anyway? They grumbled, but the fight Kila had hoped to instigate didn't erupt.

The tarp came off her and hands gripped her elbows. Suddenly she was airborne. She landed with a grunt as a man's shoulder pressed into her gut. She was being carried like a sack of potatoes.

The sounds of the world went quiet as they passed through a door.

"Put her down." It was Dunne Marlow's voice. There was some clinking. A purse full of gold. Kila got a glimpse of the glow and coughed in astonishment. Five hundred hadn't been a far-off guess. She spotted four gold citadels and a whole bunch of skillets. The door slammed shut.

The hood came off her head with a whoosh. She stood in a cold foyer. Not of the cathedral, though. The finely shaped stonework and dark tapestries depicting Til in all his naked and bearded glory suggested she was somewhere in the Abbey. But no way to be certain. Many people displayed such artwork, hoping to convince the Donse Masters of their piety. Funny, that. In Kila's experience, Donse Masters measured piety in coin, not by one's decor.

She slipped the queller back on. The world seemed to dim. But if this was the Abbey, she didn't want to risk the Hargothe coming back into her mind. "Untie my hands."

"No."

"Then take me to the Hargothe and let's be done with it."

"Not yet."

"So now what?"

He approached her, and she noticed the net over his shoulder. He set it down and loosened the top. Nax hopped out. The little gray looked a bit ruffled, but not injured.

"We wait."

"I'm hungry."

"Food will be brought."

"Where are we?"

He didn't answer except to offer a tight-lipped smile.

"Is it true about you and the Spinster?" she asked, hoping to get some sort of reaction from him.

The man paused, smile faltering. "So, Grig couldn't keep his mouth shut after all."

"Don't be too disappointed in him. He's merely stupid."

There was a padded bench along one wall. The table next to it held a mercus lamp. A heavy oak door stood opposite. Nax nosed it then returned to sit on Kila's bare feet, hissing when Dunne Marlow approached.

"Easy, Beloved One. I merely seek to relieve Miss Sigh of this blade." With swift tugs and yanks he undid the sheathe buckles on her leg. Kila considered kicking him in the head, but given the poor effect Cayne had on his weirdly hard flesh, she resisted.

He shook his head and muttered to himself as he placed the weapon on a side table. Taking a seat, he folded his hands in his lap. "Perhaps I *will* tell you about the Spinster. It's a rather good story, and I've never told it. What with it being the source of my disgrace and all."

The door swung open to admit a man in livery bearing a tray. Though her mercus senses were quelled, the smell of bread and soup made Kila's stomach rumble. Nax meowed. The man halted mid-step, mouth agape at the sight of the cat.

"Never mind the animal, man," Dunne Marlow said. "Set the tray down and leave."

The man obeyed but gave Nax a judgmental sneer before retreating the way he'd come. Kila eyed the loaf of bread. "You'll have to unbind my hands if I'm going to eat."

"Fear not. I have hands for the two of us." He broke off a small bit and held it out. "Don't bite me."

For a flash of an instant, her mind faltered as she watched his fingers extend with the bread. It seemed oddly familiar. But off.

"Is something wrong?" Marlow asked, still proffering the bread.

"No. I just had the odd feeling that I've done this before. Like 'Memories to Come.' The old song."

He squinted at her. "I know it well. Will you eat?"

She opened her mouth and he stuffed the bread in. She barely managed to stifle a moan of pleasure as she chewed the warm, soft bread. Instead, she closed her eyes and sighed through her nose. This wasn't the nasty rye baked in Cheapsgate ovens. This was soft, buttery, and faintly sweet.

"Spin Hetta was a bit older than you," Dunne Marlow said. "Perhaps eighteen when I met her the first time. I was a full acolyte in my third year, just twenty-one. But the Spinsters have a different system than the Way of Til. Those who ascend in the sister-hood do so by lottery, not seniority or merit." He waved a finger at her. "But don't for one moment think they are dimwitted. Hetta was the wisest girl I ever knew. You could look into her eyes and glimpse the divinity of Pol herself."

Kila smirked and raised an eyebrow. "I thought the Way of Til didn't accept the goddess of Luck as fully divine."

Dunne Marlow took a bite of bread, then offered Kila another. She accepted, eagerly.

He stood and stretched. "It's chilly in here. I wonder what's keeping the lad."

Having no idea what he was talking about, Kila didn't offer any speculations.

"The New Pantheon is all gibberish," Dunne Marlow said. "The synod that decided the order of things—even the names of the gods themselves—were a bunch of drunk old men and women lusting for power beneath the radiance of Her Enlightened Majesty. It is, as I believe they say in Cheapsgate, a load of bilge water. But that is not pertinent to this discussion. My dear Hetta was wise, young, and a full Spinster in the Way of Pol. You might be interested to know that she had some facility with the mercus. Nothing compared to you, I'm sure, but I can count the Donse Masters who could have matched her on these three fingers." He made the sign of the trident at her, tucking pinky and thumb.

Kila instantly grew curious. She wanted to know the names of those Donse Masters. "The Hargothe is one. Who are the other two?"

Dunne Marlow grinned, and she saw some of the boy in him. His salt-and-pepper hair was overlong at the front, and dangled in his eyes. He had a habit of tossing his head to swing his bangs out of the way. "The Hargothe is not a Donse Master. And as for the others . . . Dunne Chilow is dead. The second is Dunne Yples, of late committed to a dungeon cell. That was your fault, by the by. The last one I'm too modest to mention."

Kila let out a snort. He was talking about himself, of course. But that bit about Dunne Yples stuck in her brain. "What did I do that sent a Donse Master to a prison cell?"

"You drove him mad. He was in the thinnie cavern when you did . . . whatever it was that you did. For someone unprepared for such a release of power, the effects can be quite disturbing. The Ways have lost many mercusine talents once taught to children, you know. One of which is shielding against such feats as yours. Alas, poor Yples is quite mad now. My little mice tell me he raves about you in his cell, denouncing you as Dem-Kisk."

Kila pursed her lips as she took in this torrent of information. A chill worked its way along her arms and she grew suddenly light-headed.

Every child knew the word Dem-Kisk. No one

would want it used in the same sentence as their name. Mouth dry and heart thumping, she cleared her throat. "I didn't—I didn't see a Donse Master there."

That wasn't true at all. She remembered one. Finta Sahng was being traded to the Hargothe in return for the services of a Donse Master. Kila had run right past the man on her way to save Nax from drowning.

She had forgotten all about him. He had surely seen what she'd done.

"Spin Hetta brought out the best in me, despite what has been said about my shame. My detractors attribute all my transgressions to her physical beauty —which was great, make no mistake—but it was her *way of being* that drew me to her. She lived effortlessly, or so it seemed to me. Her spirit was as lithe as her body. She could focus all her considerable mental powers on any task she chose, then let the concentrations of the day slide away and enjoy a hearty laugh and a lovely sunset. Her knowledge of bawdy jokes was limitless, and she reveled in my prudish blushes."

Kila couldn't concentrate on Marlow's words. If Dunne Yples had seen her kill all those people . . . then perhaps his talk about Dem-Kisk was not the joke Marlow made it out to be.

"I loved her. I'll admit it. My vows to Til were like stick soldiers against the War Captains of Starside. They fell to pieces and were forgotten in the same instant. The Spinsters accept men into their order, though few choose that path. I asked the Coin to admit me. She tossed the medallion but it came up frowns. My request was denied. In defiance of my Way, I went to Hetta and asked her to marry me. She spun her own medallion and it came up grinning. She accepted. What followed was the most sublime ten-day of my life."

Dunne Marlow returned to the bench and plopped his weight onto it. His eyes glistened. He said nothing more.

15

THE FIFTH ENLIGHTENED

The Citadel of Her Enlightened Majesty was a single massive structure set upon the slopes of the Honor Mountains. But once inside, a visitor discovered it to be a compound of separate buildings inside a thick protective curtain wall. All were fortified with parapets, portcullises, and archer windows. All were dwarfed by the royal residence and tower.

The Hargothe saw none of this, for he was blind. The steward who escorted his sedan chair kept up a running narrative of what was around them. The Hargothe tuned him out. He rested upon the mercusine, feeling for the presence of the most powerful person in the Divided City. Her Enlightened was purported to have more mercus power than all Donse Masters combined.

The Hargothe doubted this, for he had never once

felt her presence. He supposed she might have Marlow's trick of masking herself. But even so, why had she not flared upon the mercusine even once?

No. She must be very weak, perhaps devoid of the power entirely. Her title had been inherited, so the Hargothe supposed she was not enlightened at all, but merely a woman.

Still, she possessed actual physical power through her command of armies, the Watch, and her Fell Guard. To her, the Highest, the Voluptuary, and the Coin were subjects to be ordered about the same as she would order a maid to empty her chamber pot.

"I'm afraid your chair can go no further, Seer Hargothe," the steward said. He smelled soapy, but also nervous. The Hargothe grazed the man's mind with calm. The man continued, softly, "I've sent ahead for a smaller conveyance. Palace servants will carry you the rest of the way to Her audience chamber."

The Hargothe felt his attendants stiffen. He waved them to silence and ease. "That will be well."

The new conveyance was a smaller chair. The Hargothe found it rather uncomfortable, as it was not sufficiently padded. He did not complain.

He resumed his meditations upon the mercusine as he was carried into the palace. The air turned warm, and the sounds of stamping atlens and marching patrols faded to stillness. The air was spiced of cinnamon and apples. It reminded him of his youth on the farm. Not particularly good memories. But his father's short temper and heavy hand had shaped him and Marlow into the men they were.

Father had died knowing his own son was sending waves of terror into his brain until his heart gave out. A satisfying day, that had been.

"And here we are, Seer Hargothe," the steward said. "We will withdraw."

His chair was set down and the sounds of feet and robes swishing faded to his left. A door shut with a soft clunk. The Hargothe felt the room with his senses. Large, muffled by tapestries and carpets, he imagined. Two guards remained, standing utterly still except for the breath passing through their nostrils. Fell Guards, certainly. He had seen them before he'd put out his eyes. More imposing warriors were not to be found, dressed as they were in burnished gold breastplate, scarlet capes, and atlen-plumed helms. A single man of the Fell Guard was said to be worth a hundred of the Watch.

"I imagined you to be much older." The woman's voice startled him. Either she had come in silently, or she had been here all along. Either way, he couldn't suppress the unsettled feeling that moved across his skin. Had she been studying him even as he had been studying the room?

There wasn't the slightest mercus spark in her. She was void of the power or she was masked.

"I am nearly seventy, Your Enlightened Majesty," he said. "Practically a fledgling. Forgive me for not making the proper obeisance. I am quite unable to stand."

She laughed melodically. He knew well how he must appear. An emaciated corpse of a man. Surely he looked two hundred years old if a day.

"Have you come bearing new prophecy, Seer Hargothe?"

"Yes. I have seen the threat of danger over the Citadel. It comes in the form of a raven."

Silence.

No, not total silence. A slight rub of fabric on fabric. A soft tap. Was it a goblet being set upon a table?

"A raven, you say?" Her voice was melodic, with a breathy quality in it. She sounded just as one might expect a twenty-five-year-old woman to sound. "That's odd. My insignia is the Raven-in-Fight. What tells you the raven of your vision signifies danger?"

"Prophecy comes as it comes, Your Enlightened Majesty. Til shows what He shows. The visions are not meant as warnings, but to remind us of His power when we see the prophecy is fulfilled."

"I see. Of course, that is the doctrine."

"But as the Enlightened, you already knew of the raven, didn't you?"

"Impertinent question, Seer Hargothe. But I'll allow it. I do get so few interesting guests. I'll admit I've long been curious about you. Whether you existed or not."

"The Hargothe does not always exist."

She let his comment go, which surprised him. He didn't fail to notice that she had not answered his question.

She emanated a feeling of boredom now. He couldn't quite place what told him that. A smell? A change in the cadence of her breathing. She was damnably frustrating.

She said, "So . . . you have told me of the raven. Surely you could have sent a message."

"There is another matter, Your En—"

"Majesty will do. Your throat does sound dry. Would you like wine?"

"No, Majesty. Thank you. There is another matter."

"Go on."

Her voice was quite lovely. He thought she kept it soft for his benefit. Or perhaps so the guards could not hear.

"There is a man of great wisdom who would be a valuable counselor to you here in the Citadel."

"I have two Donse Masters spying on me already, Seer Hargothe."

"Majesty, my position obliges me to object. The Way of—"

"Spare me your defenses, Seer. Who is this man? What are his qualities?"

"He is Dunne Marlow. He is of a different stripe than other Donse Masters. Trained at the Abbey, powerful in the mercus, and quite skilled at turning up information others want kept secret."

"Why in the name of the Triumvirate would I want such a man near me?" she said, laughing softly. "He sounds quite dangerous."

The Hargothe grimaced at her use of "Triumvirate," a reference to the Three Siblings as co-equal. The Way of Til did not use that word. Ever. He let it go. "Marlow can be relied on to serve you loyally, and with no question of betraying your confidences."

"That is a bold assertion. But I do not fear betrayal. It is foolish to fear that which is certain to occur. Perhaps it will not be Dunne Marlow who betrays me, but someone will. Someone always does."

She was speaking of the history of assassination in the Citadel. As the Fifth Enlightened Majesty, she knew well the fate of her predecessors. Murdered, every single one.

Before the Hargothe could offer more assurances, she spoke. "I will add your man to my advisory staff. For a ten-day. If I am satisfied, he will be retained. If not . . . the Divide is a long, lonely walk."

The Hargothe clamped his lips shut. He wanted to smile. He liked this woman, despite himself. He understood now why she had so successfully consolidated her power. "Then I have nothing else to say."

"But I do."

"Majesty?"

"I want to discuss the girl you hunt. I want to discuss Kila Sigh."

The Hargothe was accustomed to discomfort. His whole life was discomfort. But this was something new. He felt like Father had caught him cutting up one of the chickens—a favorite pastime when he was young. A wave of guilt hit him, followed by rigid defiance.

"Who?" he said.

"Surely you've felt her upon the mercusine. Like a flare-star in the winter sky."

He felt a wash of air across his face as she stood. Her footsteps were slight scuffs, slippers upon a plush rug. Her voice came from behind him. "The Coin came to me just two days ago to discuss her."

The Coin. How that old biddy continued to breathe after all these years was a mystery. Talk about Pol's own luck. But then, one did not become Coin without enjoying a very long streak of eerie luck. Medallion toss after medallion toss going in your favor. "I have felt the presence." He would admit nothing more. "Did the Coin ask your assistance in apprehending the girl?"

"On the contrary, she asked me to leave her be. It seems the medallion spun seven frowns in a row when asked whether the girl must captured."

Spinsters! Superstitious hags, all of them. No better than the harlots of Ori in the Hargothe's estimation.

"Are you not well?" the Enlightened asked, a true

note of concern in her voice. The Hargothe realized he'd been wheezing.

"Quite well, Majesty. I concur with the Coin, though we have not discussed it. Has the Voluptuary offered counsel on the topic?"

"She has not. She had the girl in her charge for a while, but she let her go. I find that curious, don't you?"

He did. He did indeed. What was that woman playing at? With a girl like Kila Sigh in her control, the Voluptuary's influence might rival the Highest of Til's. It was not like the woman to relinquish such advantage.

"The girl has disappeared from the mercusine," he said. "Perhaps she has left Starside. That might be best."

"Yes. That might be. After what she did to the thinnies, I think her quite dangerous. I'd rather she leave the city than fall into the wrong hands."

"Then we are in accord."

"Shall I call for servants to carry you out now?"

"Please, Your Enlightened Majesty. I do grow weary."

The servants fetched him and took him from the palace. He sighed with relief once transferred to his own sedan chair. As exhausted as he was, he did not sleep on the ride back to the Abbey. He sifted the mercusine for the slightest sniff of Kila Sigh.

Nothing.

16

SHADLINE OR NO

Kila was vaguely aware that Dunne Marlow's mood had shifted. He hadn't spoken since stopping his story about Spin Hetta. His eyes glistened. His habitual smile never left his lips, but now his face was tired and sad.

"Will they kill my cat?" she asked. "I'll do anything you want, just let Nax go."

He regarded her a moment. "You weren't listening, where you? I told you something I've told no one else. But I suppose I shouldn't be surprised. You do have more pressing concerns than learning about my painful past. Frankly, I don't know what will happen to your cat. Much depends on what happens next. The Hargothe has made me a very attractive offer in exchange for you and your animal. But as I'm sure you will appreciate, if one person values something then it is very likely that others do."

"What's the offer? Maybe I can match it?"

"Unless you can get me assigned to a council position in the Citadel, I'm afraid you have nothing to offer." He rubbed his chin and gave her a rueful look. "But I know the Hargothe well. I know how he thinks. He will meet the terms of our bargain, but do so in a way that advantages him and spites me. He can't help himself. He was always vain, jealous, and convinced that others' successes robbed him of something."

Kila knew the type. She also knew Dunne Marlow's type. Part of her could respect the game he played. Life was all about trade. People with nothing to trade ended up themselves being traded. That's why Father had taught her and Wen to steal.

"Do you need anything stolen?" she asked.

Marlow grunted a laugh. "You may recall I have other agents at my disposal who can steal with impunity."

The door swung open, admitting a burst of cold air from outside. Dunne Marlow stood, gave a slight bow. "Highest, thank you for agreeing to see me."

There was only one man in the Abbey who would go by the title of Highest. This was Nare Binel, recently raised to the most powerful post in the Way of Til. In Starside, at least.

Kila didn't keep track of which Nares sat at the Thebkine Table. But Fallo had recently mentioned that this man was his uncle. She'd expected someone older. But Highest Binel was nowhere near forty. His sandy hair was cut short and swept back from his high fore-head. If it hadn't been for the brown frock worn by all Donse Masters, he might've been dashing. The vestments of his rank were not upon his shoulders. And he was alone, which was unusual for a man of his position.

Kila's instincts told her this meeting was unofficial. Besides, Dunne Marlow was a disgraced Donse Master, expelled from the order. The Highest of Til could not meet with such a man.

The man had soft brown eyes, which gave him a naturally placid expression. He betrayed no shock at the sight of the cat resting on Kila's feet. His fingers were heavy with gold rings. Kila guessed he had five gold skillets' worth on each hand. But the value of these items would be many multiples of that. One in particular, the Highest's seal, would command a thousand gold skillets. Perhaps ten times that to the right buyer, who for a short time could forge documents in the Highest's name.

"Scrawny thing, isn't she?" the man said. He spoke like a Gristensider. "I don't know what I expected. Given her powers, something a bit more . . ."

"Manly?" Kila offered.

Highest Binel drew in a sharp intake of breath, then smiled. "I was going to say 'forbidding.' But look at you." He folded his hands inside the cuffs of his robe. With slow steps he paced in front of her, eyeing the boyish clothes she had stolen, and sparing the slightest glance for Nax.

He smells strange, Nax sent. There was an undercurrent of tension in the sending.

Incense.

"You risk much bringing her to me like this," the Highest said to Dunne Marlow. "What's stopping me from just taking her from you?"

"You know," Marlow said.

The Highest clenched his jaw and narrowed his eyes. "Yes of course. The Hargothe. I owe my position to him. But still, I could take her and the animal and present them to the Hargothe. That would earn me his favor, and you nothing."

Marlow shrugged. "By all means, do that. And while you're at it, congratulate yourself for taking advantage of my idiocy. Of course I would bring her here with no contingency to protect me. And of course you would just tell me you're going to steal from me. Can we please dispense with this banter? I came to strike a deal."

Instead of flying into the rage Kila expected, Highest Binel laughed. "It's good to see you again, Dunne Marlow. I've missed our talks. Your brother is . . . how can I say this . . . not a noted conversationalist."

Now it was Dunne Marlow's turn to laugh. He turned to the tray and plucked up a goblet. "Wine?"

"No thank you." The Highest turned his attention back to Kila. "I'm sure you recognize that turning her over to the Hargothe comes with risks. The question was raised at the Thebkine Table that she may be Dem-Kisk. It hardly seems likely that she is the one. But on the other hand, one would hardly expect the Dem-Kisk to arrive on a black stallion, accompanied by nosgkin trumpeters. I deferred the question to the Garden. And your brother is meeting with Her Enlightened as we speak."

"He is, is he?" Dunne Marlow said, nodding slowly. "Interesting. Perhaps he's more desperate for her than I thought."

Kila wanted to crawl under the bench. Why did they have to start talking about Dem-Kisk? This day was getting worse and worse. Kila eyed the door. The Highest had not latched it. She needed to merely pull the handle and run.

Huff is hiding, Nax said.

What? Really? How is Henley?

Alive. Trapped in darkness. He has been hurt by the old man.

Does Huff know how to get to where Henley is?

Yes and no. Nax sent a ruffle of irritation that made heat prickle Kila's neck. Frustration.

Tell him to tell Henley I'm trying to get to him.

Her little plan to escape went out the door without her as she turned her mind to the puzzle of how to help Henley.

Dunne Marlow was speaking again. "And regardless of what you choose to do with her, my objective is the same. I wish to be reinstated as a full Donse Master and be assigned to the Citadel as a counselor to Her Enlightened Majesty. And I assure you, my brother is not discussing whether this girl is Dem-Kisk. He went to the Citadel to negotiate a position for me."

"Then we're back to the question we began with. Why are you here? What do you think I can give you that your brother cannot?"

Dunne Marlow returned to the bench and took a long sip from his goblet. He swished the wine in his mouth and swallowed. Still he didn't say anything. But the expression on his face showed no sign of him considering an answer. He seemed to be waiting.

Highest Binel must have come to the same conclusion, for he returned to his pacing, his face cast toward the floor. He mumbled to himself, "Why are you here? Why are you here? If your brother can give you the post you desire, there is no reason to risk coming here. I do have the power to reinstate you. And I certainly have the power to get you the position you wish." He turned toward Kila. "But why does the Hargothe want this girl so badly?"

"To use her as he uses the others you allow him?" Marlow said.

"We do send him the occasional boy to drain. He's quite occupied with one in particular right now. Usually they don't last more than a few minutes. But this one has endured two sessions, and yet he still breathes." Binel shuddered and rubbed his elbows.

Huff says we should go far away. Nax's feelings were clearly aligned with Huff's. And so were Kila's. She knew better than to ask Nax how far away Huff was. But if they could converse here, it surely meant Kila was in the Abbey. That meant she was close to Henley.

Marlow broke the silence that had begun to stretch between him and the Highest. "The Hargothe's sensitivity to the mercus is a curse. It wracks his body, twists his mind, and only rarely provides him with the Seer's insights. But you know his power. You, and every Donse Master in this abbey, are subject to his mental invasions. Now imagine him strengthened, so much so he can walk about, free to meddle more."

Highest Binel made a face, as if assaulted by a bad smell. "But surely the girl is not *that* powerful. All the boys he's drained have not increased his physical vitality one bit."

"We are wasting time, Binel. I see that you are not going to come to it on your own. I'm bringing you the girl so that you can get her out of Starside. The Hargothe cannot be allowed to have her. And if she is Dem-Kisk, there is only one place for her to go."

"I see now. Send her to the Garden. Wash our hands of her entirely. And there she'll be well out of the grasp of the Hargothe, and their problem to deal with."

"That wasn't so hard, was it?"

"You are lucky you are not meeting me in an official capacity. You may have been my instructor once, but I am Highest now. Showing a little respect wouldn't kill you."

Dunne Marlow titled his head side to side as if questioning that assertion.

Kila coughed. "The girl would like to offer an opinion."

Their faces swung toward her, Marlow's amused, the Highest's indignant. Kila charged ahead, "Give me to the Hargothe."

"What?"

"What?" echoed Binel.,

What? Nax sent fear into Kila's body, and it was all she could do not to crouch and cover her head.

If we can get deeper into the Abbey, we can rescue Henley.

Who will rescue us?

Leave it to Nax to point out the stupidity of her plan. But the alternative was to be shipped off to the Garden. She would much rather take her chances here than end up on some far-flung island filled with Donse Masters, Sensuals, and Spinsters.

She pushed ahead. "But I keep my cat with me at all times." She tilted her head and glared. "Otherwise I may do to all of you what I did to the thinnies."

Highest Binel took a step back and made a ward of superstitious protection. Marlow gave her a flat stare. "Why would you suggest such a ridiculous thing?"

Kila had to admit that was a fair question. A sensible lie didn't pop into her mind so she told the truth. "The boy the Hargothe struggles with is my friend."

A splutter of laughter made Marlow's lips quiver. "And you thought you'd rescue him? Binel, did you hear that? She can't so much as make light using her power, but she thinks she can free the lad and escape."

Highest Binel did not see as much humor in it as Marlow. He pursed his lips and regarded Kila. She couldn't guess what he was thinking, but clearly some calculation was churning through his mind. When he spoke, his voice was barely a whisper. "But perhaps she might serve us after all." His eyes dropped to the table. "This is her blade?"

Marlow nodded. "Stolen, no doubt."

"It was my father's," she said. "And I want it back."

The Highest drew the blade from the sheathe and turned it in the light. "A Shadline blade. Miss Sigh, you continue to surprise me."

"She has had some training," Marlow said. "But no Shadline is she."

Kila didn't know much about Shadline blademasters, but it was obvious they recognized the quality of Cayne. She doubted it was as valuable as they speculated, else Father would have sold it long ago.

Marlow watched the Highest study the blade. Was that a look of worry on his face? "She must go the Garden, Highest. Or she must die."

"Yes. But first she can solve one of our problems,

can she not? And then the boy can return to the acolyte wards and begin his training for the Way of Til. If he has withstood the Hargothe thus far, he is surely too valuable to waste."

Kila grasped at hope. "Yes! Let me be of help. What problem do you have? I can steal anything."

Marlow's face was very grave. "It is a great risk. If she fails and he drains her . . ."

"She seems to have your skill in blocking the mercusine. He won't even know she's there."

Kila's instinct told her to be silent. Marlow's face had lost all its usual mirth. His pallor had gone quite white. He nodded once. Highest Binel turned to Kila, spun her around. He cut her bonds with Cayne, then returned the weapon to its sheathe. "We will present you to the Hargothe. And then you will kill him."

Kila's mouth went dry. When she finally managed to speak, her voice cracked. "I'll be needing my blade, then."

"Shadline or no, I will not put this weapon in your hands when I'm anywhere nearby. I'll see to it that a suitable blade comes to you when you need it."

He strode to the door, carrying Cayne with him. He glanced back to Marlow. "If she survives, we'll send her to the Garden. She may well be Dem-Kisk, after all. And as for your position in the Citadel, consider it yours."

He pushed through the door, letting icy air sweep in. Nax hissed. Kila shivered, but not from the cold.

She was used to that. "That was my father's blade. If I live, I want it back. And promise Henley will be let go, not turned into a Donse Master."

"I can make no such promises, Kila Sigh." Marlow seemed very tired now. He finished his wine and rang a bell. An acolyte bustled in, eyebrows up in question.

"Escort Miss Sigh to a private chamber. Her animal must stay with her. See that she is fed and provided a bath."

The young man absorbed these instructions with growing alarm. Disgraced or no, Marlow commanded obedience. The acolyte held the door and motioned for Kila to go in. She cast one last glance at the outer door, the final chance for freedom. But Henley was counting on her, no matter his foolish urgings for her to flee. And if she could kill the Hargothe, maybe she could find a way out and live without the fear of his thoughts ever again creeping into her mind.

"Thank you so very much, Dunne Marlow," Kila said, putting acid into her voice.

With perfect seriousness, he bowed slightly. "Thank you, Kila Sigh."

17

TWISTED SHELL

Fallo PiTorro sat on a bench beneath the Dome of the Gentle Goddess in the public Baths of Ori. The air was full of moisture, which might have been pleasant if it weren't so hot. He eyed the pools and wondered if one of them was cool. He wouldn't mind a refreshing swim.

So far he hadn't seen anyone enter any of the pools. In fact, he'd seen nobody but the rather beautiful Sensual on duty. An Iopsis woman, exotic and alluring. Except for the tight mouth of absolute disapproval and disgust she kept firmly in place. He couldn't blame her. He was as ugly as a sailor's arse boil. Or so his father had repeatedly told him all his life. Alas.

On second thought, that smirk on her face might be because of you, he sent to Lop.

The fluffy black cat lay on his lap, asleep and

making that odd buzzing sound cats made when content. He poked the plump belly. *Wake up.*

The cat's eyes slitted open. *No.* They squinted shut.

Fallo poked Lop again. *Oly has to be here. At least tell me where he is.*

Without opening her eyes, Lop sent, *I don't work for free.*

Fallo had made the tactical error of having saved a couple pieces of smoked lamb in his pocket. Lop had been surly ever since catching wind of them. Fallo knew if he rewarded the cat with a bite of it, he would pay for the information he wanted in tiny, tiny increments until the lamb was all gone.

Whose side are you on? Kila needs our help and you're standing in the way.

I'm not standing.

"You bloody well know what I mean!"

The Iopsis Sensual shushed him and gave him a death glare. He smiled and winked back at her.

If it were urgent, I would tell you, Lop sent. She stretched her foreleg until it trembled. Her fangs flashed as her jaw parted in a tongue-curling yawn.

Let me decide what's urgent, Fallo sent.

I don't trust your judgment. You always think everything is urgent. We're always running about, nearly getting killed. I think we'll follow my—

The cat shot straight up, fur out. She landed in his lap, claws digging into his thighs.

Fallo leaned back. "What the Kil-kissin' devil—?"

The cat hopped down and waddled off. *Follow, Fallo!*

With a glance at the Iopsis woman, Fallo winked and darted after Lop. The woman's indignant cries chased him as he ran between the pools and through a doorway.

And stopped dead.

A short but very serious-looking woman barred the way. Her hair was pulled back from her face and held in place by a glittering band. Fallo recognized the Voluptuary instantly. He bent a knee and swept into a courtly bow.

"None of that nonsense," she said. "Come with me."

"But my cat—"

"Will be fine. There was a little misunderstanding with Wen's cat. What an ornery monster that creature is!"

That sounded like Oly, all right. *Lop, are you still alive?*

Yes. Oly is very wet. Amusement came through the bond.

"Why is Wen's cat wet?" Fallo asked.

The Voluptuary was already striding away. "He stank. I ordered one of the novitiates to dunk him. Come with me."

Fallo obeyed. "Kila sent me. She's in trouble."

"She's Kila Sigh. She *is* trouble."

Fallo felt he should defend his friend, but he

couldn't come up with a counter-argument. The woman waved him into a side room and shut the door. It was an office, certainly not hers. A plain wooden writing desk was pushed into the corner. A single chair sat against one wall. "Sit!"

Fallo sat. The Voluptuary rounded on him, blue eyes hard, as if Kila's predicament were his fault. "Where is she?"

"The Abbey."

Whatever answer the Voluptuary had expected, the Abbey had not been it. Her face went white and she reached for the desk for support. "Impossible."

"Lop felt Nax in there. She was with a Donse Master. She passed along for me to come tell you. Do you need this chair? I can stand if you—"

The woman regained her composure by force of will. She arranged her face into her usual haughty bearing. Fallo couldn't help but notice the throb of her pulse continuing to flutter the skin at the side of her throat. "Today a demayne came into the novitiates' ward, assaulted Wen, and *dymensed* with Kila. If what you say is true, someone in the Way of Til is playing with dark forces they cannot possibly understand."

Fallo blew out his cheeks at her mention of a demayne. He wanted to plug his ears and sing a sailor's shanty to block out the rest. Only his ingrained manners kept him from doing so.

"What did you say the . . . demayne . . . did to her?"

"Dymensed!" She waved her hand irritably at his ignorance. "Vanished in mercus green to travel else-where in an instant." She snapped her fingers. "Apparently it delivered her to a Donse Master. Oh, it burns my girdle how those arse-squeezed men lecture about Til's morals. And then they trezz and wench and dabble in the blackest mercusine horrors!"

"Kila didn't mention any demayne to me. All I know is that she's been captured." He got distracted momentarily by the phrase "trezz and wench," thinking it would be fine name for a pub.

The Voluptuary was pacing now, hands clasped behind her. "I had no idea he would go to such lengths." The woman wasn't looking at Fallo anymore. She wasn't talking to him either. "Will she do as I told her?"

"I suppose it depends on what you told her to do," Fallo said. "But in my experience, Kila doesn't follow instructions very well. May I ask who 'he' is?"

The Voluptuary eyed him, seemed to be looking right through him. Fallo had only seen her from a distance in the past. Father hadn't found much use for the Sensuals of Ori in his business dealings. Donse Masters were much more susceptible to gold, and because their fingers were in every purse their whis-pers were in everyone's ears. For a merchant, good relationships within the Way of Til was good business.

Fallo didn't know what to make of the Voluptuary. Clearly she was shaken by events. But one didn't rise to the head of the Way by being timid. That meant Kila was up to her ears in it this time.

"Maybe you could help her," he said. "Go tell the Donse Masters she's a novitiate in the Way of Ori."

"They'd laugh in my face."

"Why do they want her?"

"I've said too much already. Thank you for letting me know. Return to your den in the Warren." She pulled a gold skillet from a pocket and handed it to him.

"Thank you for this. But I can't abandon Kila. Or Henley."

"Henley? As in Henley Mast?"

Fallo swallowed hard. "No. No. This is a different Henley."

She made a face and tilted her head to one side. "And I suppose you're a different Fallo PiTorro. Don't run away! I won't hand you over to your horrid father. If it's Henley Mast they have, you must tell me." The woman leaned toward him, eyes ablaze.

"Yes. He got captured a few days ago. A corpse-like man with no eyes has been torturing him. We took Henley's cat there to spy. But so far . . . a rescue plan has eluded us."

The Voluptuary absorbed this information, and a look of calculation came over her face. "How do you know about the corpse-like man? Did Kila tell you about him?"

"No. We all saw the same vision, passed from

Henley's cat to each of ours. I know it sounds mad, but it's true."

"That man you saw is the Hargothe. He is a seer, cursed with a great sensitivity to the mercusine. He seeks Kila Sigh, to what end I do not know. Likely to drain her powers. And if he is torturing Henley Mast, the boy must have mercus ability of his own."

It was Fallo's turn to absorb weird information. He had heard Kila mention having some facility with the mercus to see metals. He had dismissed it as bragging. And Henley had never once mentioned having such abilities. Fallo didn't know much about the mercus, except that Donse Masters could feel the potential for it in someone before it awakened in them. No one in his father's or mother's lines had ever possessed the spark.

"But you're the Voluptuary," he said. "You were anointed by Her Enlightened Majesty herself. Why can't you press a demand for their release, especially when you know this Hargothe bastard is torturing Henley?"

The Voluptuary's jaw set. She sighed through her nose. "The Way of Til does not accept the balance of the Triumvirate. To them, Til is Father to all. Her Enlightened tolerates this attitude in them. I do not know why. For me to go uninvited into the Abbey would only worsen tensions between the Way of Til and the Way of Ori."

"So that's it, then. It's up to me."

"Kila does have a way out, of sorts. But it won't be of any use to Henley Mast or his cat."

"What is it? If Kila can escape, we can regroup. We can think of another way to get Henley out. How much money do you think it would take to ransom him?"

The Voluptuary let out a sad laugh. "The Mast family is dead. There is no one to pay ransom. Unless you would like to go to your father and ask for the coin? I didn't think so. Though it shatters me to say it, the boy is on his own. The way out for Kila Sigh is death."

Fallo snorted and laughed. "Kil will dance with the Maidens Five in Dunne Medow Plaza before Kila Sigh will off herself. We need a better plan. What about that Alnassi woman of yours? She could beat a hundred Donse Masters to death before anyone could alert the Watch."

"You don't know what you're asking. First of all, Yiqa is not mine. Second, she would not harm a Donse Master even to save my life. She has taken oaths to defend and protect all servants of the Ways."

"But these men are corrupt. Evil."

"Perhaps. Or perhaps the Hargothe has heard the true will of Til, and his use of the boy and the girl are part of His plan. What we see as torture may be required to prevent a greater evil. I am no seer."

"Do you believe that?"

The Voluptuary answered with no hesitation.

"Don't be silly. The Hargothe is a twisted shell of a man, interested only in his own survival. But Yiqa's oaths are as resolute as the Citadel itself. She will not help you."

So that was it. Kila and Henley would get no help from the Way of Ori. Fallo stood, summoning Lop through their bond. "Thank you for caring for Wen. May I see him before I go?"

The Voluptuary's nostrils flared as she inhaled. She seemed as frustrated with the situation as Fallo was. He suspected she did not often feel helpless. "I'll have a novitiate take you to him."

18

YOU WILL KNOW DEM-KISK

If the man in the next cell was truly a Donse Master, he must've committed a terrible crime to be thrown into this dungeon. The Theb taught compassion toward the sick. To lock up a madman like Dunne Yples seemed the height of cruelty to Henley.

Not that Donse Masters were strangers to hypocrisy. More like fast friends with it, in Henley's opinion.

He propped his back against his cell door. The thick wood was slightly warmer than the stone walls. He kept his eyes closed and breathed through his teeth, which lessened the impact of the stink.

Something the madman had screamed was playing in his mind: "Thinnies in flames."

The first time he'd heard it, the words had sounded as meaningless and random as everything the man shouted. But with nothing else to do but wait for Huff to find a vantage point in the Cathedral, Henley's mind had begun connecting pieces of what the Donse Master was saying.

He screamed about "the girl." He screamed about "thinnies in flames." And above all, he screamed about "Dem-Kisk." By themselves, all ravings. But since learning from Huff that Kila had gone among the thinnies to rescue Nax, it only made sense that the girl Dunne Yples spoke of was Kila.

That left the flames and Dem-Kisk. To anyone trained in the Theb, the words went together automatically: "You will know Dem-Kisk by the flames, by the charred bone, by the ash. You will know Dem-Kisk by the black feather, the red scale, the poison mist. You will know Dem-Kisk by the fallen tower, the creaking gate, the bone chill."

It was the most cryptic passage in the Theb, and the subject of endless trezz-fired speculations. One of Henley's tutors, Spinster Bligh, had called it "fortuneteller's stew," from which one could draw any conclusion. She had dismissed the notion of its prophecy, and pointed out that the word Dem-Kisk meant, literally, "red grass" in the ancient tongue of the elnisians.

"Red could mean 'blood,'" Henley had said.

The woman had arched an eyebrow. "Or it could refer to the wheat crops of Cigil-Tine's fields, depicted in paintings and tapestries always as crimson."

Henley had then questioned the passage's presence

in the Theb. If it meant nothing, then perhaps the rest of the book meant nothing. Spin Bligh—a plain, pale woman with eyes too close together—had leveled a beady stare at him and said, "Don't be a silly goose."

Without warning, and without Henley opening his eyes, vision flooded his mind. He saw the nave of the Cathedral from the vantage of the pulpit. Huff had finally slunk up there, and was now sharing the catsight. For once, Henley was thankful he hadn't eaten much. His stomach quavered as his vision contradicted the orientation of his head.

Do you see? Huff sent.

I see. The black altar stood on the dais directly below. Behind it was screen of woven gold bars, beyond which stood the Thebkine Table. In the shadows to the right of the screen was a wrought-iron railing. It surrounded an opening in the floor where a staircase descended to the crypts.

Henley turned his head, but the vision didn't track. Instead of telling Huff where to look, Henley focused his attention on the staircase opening. *Do you see it?*

Huff moved his head, centering the opening in his vision. *There?*

Yes. They took me down there.

Someone's coming! The catsight vanished.

Wait! Henley sent.

No response. Henley pressed his palms to his face. *Huff, don't go down there.*

No response. He felt the cat's presence on the

move. He focused on that, but found it impossible to gauge distance.

Huff. What's going on?

No response. And then, *Kila is here.*

Where are you? Are you hiding?

Annoyance flowed through the bond. *No, I've jumped into a Donse Master's lap.* The tone was perfect sarcasm. *Were you listening? Kila is here.*

Henley let go of the tension in his body. But not before sending a dose of it through the bond. *I heard you. Where is she?*

The catsight returned. The vantage was from the floor, looking up. Kila was like a giant looking down at him. Nax rested on her shoulders. Behind her was a tapestry, a table, and the edge of a cot. The catsight vanished.

Kila says she's going to try to get you out. But first she has to kill someone called the Hargothe.

19

CACOPHONY OF TERROR

Dunne Marlow may have influence over acolytes, but his orders to provide Kila with a bath did not produce the steaming copper tub she had envisioned. Not that she relished the idea of bathing in the Abbey. But when an acolyte brought in a small basin of tepid water, she couldn't help but feel slighted.

The bread was good, however. She had eaten all of it within minutes, then scooped the remaining butter onto her finger and swallowed that, too.

The acolyte who brought in the tray had not noticed the orange cat slipping in behind him. Huff had slunk under the cot and wisely remained there until the acolyte departed. Kila barely mastered her own astonishment at the sight of him. Nax didn't react at all. Of course, Nax had known Huff was coming and had failed to mention it to Kila.

She knelt and extended her hand, palm up. Huff approached with tentative steps, sniffed her fingertips, then accepting a scratch on the chin.

Henley wants you to stay away from the old man, Nax sent, relaying Huff's words. *He can get into your mind.*

Tell Henley I know that. I can keep him out.

Henley says you are stubborn and will certainly die. A flush of heat—Nax's disapproval—accompanied this statement.

Kila was used to being called stubborn. She knew it wasn't intended as a compliment, but she chose to hear it as such. *Tell Henley I came down two flights of stairs from the cathedral. I turned left, and was taken to a room on the left.*

Henley says he's deeper beneath the Cathedral. He thinks. But he is sure he is on the same level as the old man. He says you should escape. The old man tortures the mind.

Tell him I felt it. We all felt it.

Henley says, "in that case, you're even stupider than I thought."

Kila eyed Nax. "Henley did not say that."

She sat on the cot and patted it. Huff hopped up next to her and allowed her to stroke his body and tail. Nax nosed Huff, sniffed under his tail, then curled up in a ball. *Huff is hungry.*

Kila didn't have any food. She doubted the acolytes would bring her meat. Even if she could ask them. She'd heard the lock mechanism scratch closed when the last one had left.

Henley says the old man is in a tomb. There is a banded door at the end of a corridor which leads to the prison. Henley's cell is locked.

Kila didn't have Father's lock-picking tools. They were with Wen, most likely. *Ask him if the lock is metal.*

He doesn't know. Nax was getting impatient relaying messages. The cat covered her eyes with a paw.

Kila busied herself with the tepid water and soap, cleaning her face and hands, then giving her feet a good scrub-down. The water turned black.

The lock on her door scratched and squeaked.

Tell Huff to hide, she sent.

The door opened. A Donse Master stepped in. The man was young, round-faced, cheeks splotchy. He closed the door, observed Nax for a moment, then turned his attention to Kila. "Highest Binel sent me. I'm to present you to the Hargothe."

Kila's heart started ramming her ribcage. She sent a nudge to Nax, who woke up and jumped to the floor at her feet. "Did you bring me something?" Kila asked, extending her hand. "From Highest Binel?"

"I was not instructed to bring you anything. Come with me."

He turned his back on her. The temptation to take him down, the way she'd taken down so many marks on the street, pulled at her. She took two quick steps forward but stopped at the last moment. The young

Donse Master had opened the door, and she saw two strong acolytes waiting in the hallway.

She followed the Donse Master. The acolytes followed her. Nax climbed to her shoulder. She heard muttering behind her, causing her to turn. "She's not a demayne. Just an animal. A very special animal."

"Silence," the Donse Master said. The acolytes said nothing more.

Down stairways, through corridors, and then to another stairway that wound down and down and down. The way was marked by whale-oil lanterns, which surprised Kila. Why wouldn't they use mercus light here? But then she thought, why waste it in the bowels of the Abbey when the mercus power could be sold to Radiants in Gristenside?

They joined an elderly man, thin of body, but with jowls that drooped like a turkey's. He looked as old as Finta Sahng. He muttered under his breath as he led the Donse Master into darkness. He carried a lantern, spindly arm held high before him. The orange light bled into the shadows, illuminating ranks of tombs. They passed alcove after alcove, each containing a stone sarcophagus. The lids were sculpted with effigies of the Donse Masters that lay dead within, the stolid faces staring into eternity with unblinking eyes. Kila shivered and looked away.

The old man abruptly stopped and turned to a plain wooden door. He held his finger to his lips. "Absolute silence."

The Donse Master stopped the man from opening the door. "Highest Binel instructed me to take the girl in alone."

"That's absurd. No stranger goes into the Hargothe's presence without guards."

The Donse Master looked at the acolytes. He blinked several times before nodding. "Very well. Proceed."

The old man opened the door, stepped in. The Donse Master followed. The acolytes nudged Kila forward.

The first thing she noticed was the smell. Stale urine, and beneath that the thick stench of darker excretions. The air was hot, filled with moisture. No decorations relieved the stark tomb. The walls were stone block, curving into a low arch overhead.

Kila had never feared small spaces—she loved them usually—but his chamber felt tight, heavy. As if the ceiling and walls might collapse inward at any moment.

I smell death, Nax sent.

The elderly servant was leaning over the bed, the only piece of furniture in the room. He had hung the lantern on a wall hook. The light cast his shadow over the bed.

Whispers filled the chamber, like the secret murmurings of snakes. The old servant straightened, nodded to the round-faced Donse Master, and led him from the room.

The door closed behind them.

Kila stood three paces from the bed. A corpse lay upon it. Incredibly, it lived. The movements of its chest lifted the bedsheet in slow intervals. Each inhale and exhale sent up a papery rasp from thin, cracked lips. The white sheet was drawn up to the corpse's chin. The eyes were open, exposing empty sockets.

"I can't feel you," the corpse said. "But I can smell you."

The head turned toward her, fixing its black void gaze upon her. "You have learned a trick of the mercus few know." The sunken cheeks pulled the lips tight. The corpse-man's mouth gaped, and the lantern light illumined brown teeth. This was the face she had seen in Henley's vision. This was the face of horror. This was the Hargothe.

She unwittingly retreated a step and bumped into an acolyte. The man shoved her forward. Kila barely noticed, for all her attention was focused on the Hargothe. That someone could survive in such a frail state . . . The empty eyes remained fixed on her, violating her with their naked emptiness.

Highest Binel had promised that a blade would be available when she needed it. So where was it? She licked her lips, but her dry tongue couldn't moisten them. She glanced at one acolyte, then the other. Their faces were stony, eyes fixed ahead.

"I taste the soap on you," the Hargothe said. "But also the stink of Cheapsgate. Perhaps you are not Kila

Sigh. . . . But no, I smell the Beloved One. I've handled many of them in my day. What color is it?"

Kila wasn't about to answer this question. Her hand went to Nax's head.

"One of you acolytes," the old man hissed. "Tell me."

The one to Kila's left cleared his throat. "Charcoal gray, white feet."

"Lovely. And dangerous. Do you know why there is a bounty on these animals, girl?" He didn't wait for her response. "They are Beloved of Kil, and as such are despised by Til. They are infested with the spirits of demayne."

"I've seen a demayne," Kila said. "Such a creature could not fit in a little cat."

The Hargothe started to make a rasping noise. For a moment, Kila thought he was choking. The lips spread wide, his skin tightened, showing shape of his skull quite clearly. His lower jaw jiggled up and down. He was laughing.

"You are ignorant," he wheezed. "Amusing, but ignorant. Acolytes, draw her arms behind her."

No sooner were the words in the air than the two men had gripped Kila by the elbows and wrists. With a jerk, they pulled her arms behind her, straining her shoulders. She gritted her teeth, refusing to let out the moan of pain that rose in her throat.

Nax drove her claws into Kila's flesh lest she be spilled to the floor.

"They have the strength to dislodge your shoulders. I understand it is quite painful. Drop your shield to the mercus, or they will hurt you. And that will be but the beginning of your agonies."

Kila's mind raced. There was no weapon here. The Highest had betrayed her. She had no chance of muscling away from these two acolytes.

Her father's advice popped to mind. *You cannot stop the tide. Swim with it.*

Her voice cracked. "I have a queller. My ring."

"She does wear a ring," one of the acolytes said.

"Remove it!" the Hargothe said.

Thick fingers pinched the ring and yanked it from Kila's hand. The zing of awakened mercus senses washed over her. The reek of the room made her gag. Not just stale urine, but the rotten exhalations of the Hargothe filled the air with a miasma of decay. A trickle of water sounded all around. As the room brightened to her sharpening sight, she noticed channels cut in the stone floor where water coursed. Steam wafted upwards from it, forming a wispy mist that reached her knees.

The Hargothe's voice burst into her mind. *There you are!*

She wanted to thrust it out, but she had no concept of how to do so. She could no more keep the Hargothe's greedy thoughts from fingering her brain than she could push the wind away from her.

Nax hissed. Her fur stood straight out.

The Hargothe cackled. "Bring the girl to my bedside."

The acolytes lifted her, carried her three paces, then set her feet onto the floor next to the bed. One of them shoved a foot into the back of her knee, forcing her to kneel. The other man pushed the back of her head until her forehead pressed into the stinking mattress.

"Place my hand," the Hargothe said.

The meaty strength of the acolyte's hand was replaced by the featherlight touch of the Hargothe's. Kila tried to cringe away, but she was held fast by the two strong men. Nax spat as she scurried from Kila's shoulder and under the bed.

A sensation like ants crawling over her skin erupted *inside* her head. The Hargothe probed with his mercus senses. She squeezed her eyes shut as he combed her mind, greedily seeking purchase. Gritting her teeth, she moaned and sought a way—any way— to resist. But she didn't know how.

The Hargothe's slithery voice came into her thoughts. *Ha, I've found the bond with the Beloved One. Just like the boy. He survived my explorations, and he's much weaker than you. Let's see what we can see.*

Pain sprouted in Kila's head. Like a nail driven through one temple and straight out the opposite side. A scream ripped from her throat. Her body flailed of its own accord, futile against the strength of the acolytes. They leaned against her, using their weight to hold her in place. The Hargothe's hand burned her scalp.

The stabs and fires of agony suddenly withdrew and quenched. She shuddered in relief for one heartbeat, two.

And then came the pain again, skewering her from temple to temple. Another pierced straight into the crown of her head, while yet another thrust from the base of her skull near her spine upward toward her eyes. Each added its own infinite agony, making colors flare in her vision, shrieks tore from her mouth, and vomit gurgled in the back of her throat.

Inside, she recoiled from the torture, seeking any haven, any respite no matter how small.

She discovered that a tiny spot of calm existed within the cacophony of terror. The bond with Nax. Kila clung to it, the way she might cling to a high ledge while her feet hung over emptiness.

I'm here, Nax sent. *I'm here.*

20

———

SOMEONE STUPID

enley awoke to screaming. Dunne Yples was back at it. "Dem-Kisk! Dem-Kisk!"

Henley wiped slobber from his lips and found it was more than saliva. The stinking bitter flavor of bile made him lean over and spit.

The pain had come on instantly, passed from Kila to Nax to Huff to him. He shivered, recognizing the hateful touch of the Hargothe.

SOMEONE WAS HELPING Fallo to his feet. He blinked away the tears in his eyes, shook off the hands that were tugging at his shoulders. On the cot in the novitiates' ward of the Baths of Ori, Wen shuddered with convulsions. A blond novitiate girl leaned close to him, calling his name and begging for him to calm.

Suddenly he did. Oly leapt onto his chest and turned to hiss at the girl.

Fallo turned to see who had been helping him. He instantly recognized Raginalt Keel, the youngest son of Hackworth Keel.

Ragin recoiled, mouth dropping open. "Fallo PiTorro? But you're dead!"

Fallo sent to Lop, *Tell Oly to relax.* Oly stopped hissing, but he didn't move from his protective position on Wen's chest. He did allow the girl—a novitiate as beautiful as Fallo was hideous—to pat Wen's face. Wen's eyes flickered open.

Fallo nodded a greeting to Ragin. "I *am* dead. And I ask to stay that way."

A dawning of understanding came over Ragin's face. "I've had a falling out with my own father. I understand."

"It wasn't a falling out. My father tried to have me murdered. And why are you here?"

Ragin's shoulder's slumped. "I showed an enemy mercy."

Fallo felt the lovely girl's eyes on him. She was glaring and holding a finger to her mouth. Wen had gone to sleep.

"What happened?" she whispered. "We found you writhing on the floor, screaming your bloody head off." Her eyes darted from Oly to Lop. "It was these accursed animals, wasn't it?"

Fallo didn't know how to explain what he had felt,

what he had seen. The same thing that had happened to Henley before. A catsight vision of the old man, and then the pain. But this time it had happened to Kila. And it had been so much worse.

"The cats didn't do it," Fallo said. "Something happened to one of our friends, and the cats passed it along to us."

"One of your friends. You mean Kila." The girl's eyebrows bunched up and the sides of her mouth turned down. "Wen doesn't need any more pain. He was upon the River Lumne already when his ragamuffin sister dragged him here. She should leave him be."

She had a lot of nerve blaming Kila, Fallo thought. He was about to declare his opinions when Wen spoke. "It's not Kila's fault." His voice was raspy and weak. Sweat beaded on his brow, and his lips were tinged with blood. "Leave us, Darya," Wen said to the girl. "You, too, Ragin. I need to speak with Fallo alone."

Ragin and Darya left, but not without him casting back a curious glance and her a mistrustful one. When the door closed, Fallo knelt next to Wen's cot. Oly had relaxed somewhat, but mostly because Lop had bullied her way onto Wen's chest. Her considerable weight didn't seem to bother Wen.

"You have to help her," Wen said. "Please." His eyes glistened. Fallo had never seen Wen healthy, but now he looked weaker than a newborn lamb.

"How?"

Wen looked away. He rested a slender hand on Oly's body. "You said you knew Highest Binel . . ."

Fallo regretted ever mentioning his uncle's name. A Donse Master's loyalty belonged to the one who held the coin. That mean Highest Binel would welcome Fallo—and he would instantly turn Fallo over to his father. That wouldn't help Kila, and it certainly wouldn't help Fallo. Or Henley. Or Wen.

"He won't help her. Not for my sake."

The room was silent except for Wen's labored breathing. Fallo wracked his brain for an alternative plan. He even considered begging his father to intercede on Kila's behalf. Not that he'd get a chance. As soon as the house guard spotted him, he'd be dragged off somewhere and cut open like a pugfish. Maybe he could get a message to his father, offer to turn himself over if Kila were freed. It was more likely Father would request Kila's head be mounted on a pike for Fallo to see.

Wen drew in a long breath. "There's something I haven't told her. I couldn't tell her. Father didn't want her to know until she was older. That was a mistake." He turned his head back, his eyes now clear. "I'm going to die, Fallo. I feel the coldness in my bones."

"You're not going to die. The Sensuals are taking good care of you. They have plenty of Finta's medicine."

"The tincture isn't a cure. You know that. I need

more every time, and I need it more frequently. Finta told me my life is waning, and there is naught she can do. You must get Kila away from that . . . thing." He lifted a trembling hand. "In my pocket." He was pointing to his clothes, neatly folded on a stool across the room.

Fallo shook out Wen's pants and dug through the pockets. He found a small roll of black canvas, neatly tied with an attached strap. "This?"

Wen nodded. "Father's lockpicking tools. Give them to my sister. There's a note inside. She'll be able to find it now."

"But Wen—"

"Help her." Wen started to cough, tongue protruding, red and thick. "Please, Fallo."

"How?"

"I don't know. But you must." Wen's eyes closed and he continued to cough and gasp. Oly nudged Lop until she moved from Wen's chest.

What now? Lop sent.

Fallo clicked his tongue as he considered the total lack of ideas in his head. Finally, he sent, *We get Kila out.*

How?

"We have to find someone to help us," he mused. "Someone stupid enough to risk his neck with no pre-planning or hope of success."

"I'm your man, then," Raginalt said. Fallo turned to see the novitiates had crept back into the room.

Darya slipped to Wen's side and took his hand. Oly gave her a suspicious glare, but she ignored it.

Raginalt waved for Fallo to follow him into the hall. "If you can get me out of here, I'll help you get Kila out of whatever mess she's in."

"Get out of here? I got in easily enough."

"Never mind. Just lead the way."

"Why would you help me?"

"Not you. Kila. I took a vow to protect her."

21

___

EDGES KEEN

Kila hadn't experienced much silence in her life. Since she could remember, she had roamed a noisy city. Even in Gristenside at night there were the occasional dog barks, the stomp of the Watch patrol, or a bell ringing out the hour. In the lulls between those sounds there was always the wind and the curl and crash of the far-off surf.

But this world, black and cold, lacked all sound. Her mind dipped beneath the surface of conscious thought, then bobbed into the air of awareness, then sank again. From silence to silence.

It was Nax who woke her. Not with a thought or a flow of sensation through their bond, but with the rough lick of her tongue against Kila's ear.

Ah, she awakens, the Hargothe said into her mind. *You should be proud of yourself. You endured tenfold what the boy did before he retreated into unconsciousness. The bond with the animal protects you. But I have felt the shape of the connection. I could sever it as easily as a seamstress cuts thread. But that's not my aim. Well, not my* sole *aim.*

Kila pushed herself up, though her arms trembled. The mercus wasn't there, and she didn't search for it. She wasn't wearing the queller, so its absence had to be due to her exhaustion. Nax's whole body shook as she took shelter under Kila.

I'm sorry, Nax.

Nax didn't respond with words. Kila sensed the animal was too scared for speaking. Kila would have been scared, too, but she had no energy left. She couldn't muster anger either. She had few choices now. None offered much of a future. Death would be merciful for both her and Nax.

A momentary brightening of the whale-oil lantern glimmered from something beneath the Hargothe's bed. She didn't need to reach for the mercus to know it was metal. Moaning, she pretended to fall forward, stretching her arm under the bed. Her fingers closed around a blade. A dagger. The steel was cold, the edges keen.

Highest Binel had said he would provide a blade. And here it was. That meant he'd known what was going to happen to her, had known she would end up on the floor. He had likely endured a similar torture at some point. No wonder he wanted the old man dead.

She drew her arm in, careful not to let the metal scrape across the floor.

"What do you want me to do?" she asked. "I'll do anything."

Kila sought strength. Clenching the hilt, she struggled to get onto her knees. The acolytes had moved to stand by the door, confident she posed no threat to the Hargothe. As weak as she was, she doubted she would get a second strike at the old man.

The Hargothe didn't answer her. A prickle of alarm came over her. She had offered surrender and he hadn't accepted. She grasped for the mercus, her hearing sharpening in an instant. Now she heard the rattle of his breath in his chest, the wheeze of every exhalation. He, too, was exhausted.

This was her moment to strike. She got a foot under her and staggered upright. The blade was pressed close to her body to hide it from the acolytes. One grunted in surprise at her sudden movement.

She knew better than to raise the knife overhead, no need. She thrust the blade point at the Hargothe's throat, just below the chin. Her arms had little strength, so she added her weight to the blow, lunging forward.

The blade struck the Hargothe's papery throat . . . and scraped away as though meeting steel armor. The blade plunged into a pillow, and Kila tumbled on top of him. The acolytes pulled her back. One gripped her wrist and twisted until her hand released the blade. It clanked onto the stone floor.

The Hargothe laughed.

You think Marlow is the only one who prepares protective wards? I learned that trick from him when we were acolytes. Now, let me see who provided the blade.

Spikes of agony pierced her brain. In moments, she heard herself screaming the name "Binel" over and over again.

She had to say nothing else, for the Hargothe ripped into her memories and pulled forth all he wished to know.

22

PUSH IT

I am outside, Huff sent. *Henley, wake up. I am outside.*

Henley!

A jolt of frustration cut into Henley's consciousness, and he jerked upright. Kila's pain had come on again, and so severely he'd convulsed on the floor. But now it was gone. Henley didn't know how long he'd been lying there, numb and thoughtless.

What happened? he asked.

Nax is gone.

Henley sensed Huff was very close by. *Where are you?*

Outside your door.

You'll be seen!

No one is out and about. I will free you.

How?

Without warning, the catsight came to Henley. He

was looking up from the floor at the outside of his cell door. A wooden bar hung from two hooks and spanned the full width of the door. There was no lock, just a thick wooden door bar.

Even if you could jump that high—

I can *jump that high.* A ruffle of indignation came through the bond.

Even so, I don't think you're big enough to dislodge the bar. You should hide before someone comes.

The catsight wavered as the cat jumped. The bar zoomed close. Henley threw up his hands, compelled by instinct to keep his face from ramming into the bar. A soft thump sounded through the door. His vision spun and the floor approached as Huff landed.

Let the catsight go! Henley sent, stomach churning. *I'm going to be sick.*

Oh. The vision vanished. *I jumped high enough. How does it work?*

Henley considered how to explain the simple mechanism of a barred door. Cats weren't particularly inclined toward even the simplest mechanical concepts.

To get the bar out, it must first go up to get it off the hooks. Show me again.

The catsight reappeared. This time Henley had braced himself for it. The oak plank was about three feet long and four inches high. The hooks holding it in place were—

The vision spun to look down the corridor, paused,

then turned back to Henley's door. *I thought I heard something,* Huff explained.

You should run.

No. It was someone screaming behind the next door.

Dunne Yples was raving again and Henley hadn't even noticed it. But it gave him an idea. *Look at the other door again.*

The vision swung. A similar bar and hooks kept Yples locked in his cell. But Huff's vantage point showed the butt end of one side of the oak plank.

Jump at that. Push it.

Huff courteously dropped the catsight. A few dull thuds sounded. Then another. Dunne Yples' screams cut off.

What's happening? Henley sent.

Why did you make me jump at that door? Now I've set loose a stinky, filthy man.

The door opened?

Yes. How do I open your *door?*

Henley pounded on his door. "Dunne Yples! Let me out! Please."

"Dem-Kisk! Dem-Kisk! Thinnies in flames! Despised of Til, begone!" Another shriek erupted, but this one high-pitched and full of pain.

Huff? Tell me what's happening.

He tried to kick me. I bit him. He fell over. I think he's dead. No, he's breathing. He stinks. A waft of what Huff smelled came through the bond. It wasn't pleasant, but no worse than the air in his cell.

"Dunne Yples. Open my door. I can help you. I'll save you from the Despised of Til." Whatever that was. Probably Huff, now that Henley thought about it.

He's standing. He's looking at your door.

"Dunne Yples, please!"

He's touching the bar on your door.

A scraping sound announced the removal of the bar. The door swung out, letting lantern light in. Henley squinted at the silhouetted bulk of the mad Donse Master. He held the door bar in his fists like a club.

Henley scrambled past him and into the corridor. He stood, grimacing as his tight legs and back muscles tried to keep him folded up.

The Donse Master grabbed a fistful of Henley's shirt. The man was two hands taller than Henley and at least triple his weight. His beard was snarled and matted with filth, as was every other inch of him. But his eyes shone. "Dem-Kisk, I tell you!"

Henley held up his hands to appear as non-threatening as possible. "I know. I heard you saying that earlier." A million times over. "The Hargothe has the girl. The one who turned the thinnies to flame."

Dunne Yples shoved Henley back and stalked down the hall, muttering, the door bar over his shoulder.

Follow me, Huff sent. *I will get us outside.*

Henley started after Yples. *Not yet. We have to get Kila free.*

But Nax is gone. Kila must be dead.

When the Hargothe . . . did what he did to me . . . you were gone, too. For a while. I won't believe Kila and Nax are dead. Not until I see them. And I could never face Wen again if I left without trying.

Nor could he look upon his own reflection. If the situation were reversed, he knew Kila would come looking for him.

23

—————

STEALTH AND TRICKERY

"You may not leave the baths without the Voluptuary's permission, Novitiate Raginalt," Sens Taht shouted. Fallo continued to the door, Ragin in tow.

The woman was standing behind her desk, fists clenched as tightly as her mouth. Ragin called over his shoulder, "Sorry, Sens Taht. I'll be back. Hopefully."

Fallo trotted across the courtyard to the Street of the Diadem. He'd never understood why the Baths were in Gristenside, seeing how they were open to all, and attracted mostly the poor from the lower slopes of Terriside. But at least the trek to the Abbey would be downhill. He was tired enough as it was, and he expected there would be more running and danger before the day was done.

"What has Kila Sigh done to us?" he said to Ragin.

"If we were smart, we'd keep going downhill and find a ship that will take us to the land of Never-Ever."

The blond boy didn't answer, but his face looked grim and determined. There was something else in it. Fallo knew that look, and he felt sorry for the lad. There was no happiness to be had falling in love with a girl like Kila Sigh. Better to find a plump, happy lass who liked a bit of wine and dancing than a scrawny thief who could turn you to ash if she got angry enough. He decided to keep his mouth shut.

A band of rain had swept in since he'd gone inside the Baths. The Citadel and the top of the Divide were hidden in mist now.

Atlen-drawn wagons and carriages trundled along the road, carrying servants toward morning markets to buy all that a Radiant's greathouse might require. None them would recognize Fallo here, but once he made it to Dunne Medow Plaza, the chances of running into merchant-class folk grew. They'd recognize Ragin, too. "We need cloaks with hoods," he said to Ragin.

"Follow me," Ragin said, striding in the wrong direction.

"The Abbey is that way." Fallo jerked a thumb downhill.

"We're not going there yet. I know someone who might help, a former novitiate. She lives in one of these houses. I'm sure she'll give us cloaks."

Like all Gristenside mansions, Radiant Peline's was

set far from the street, surrounded by a wrought-iron fence. A great gate stood open, a lone elderly guard on duty. Upon noticing Ragin's novitiates garb, he waved them through and returned to napping.

Without discussion, they headed around to the kitchen entrance. Merchants' sons knew not to go to the grand front doorway, where a butler would be apt to ring for House armsmen to put them onto the street, preferably head first.

Lop, find a bush to hide under.

It's hard to sit under your eyebrow when you're walking.

Fallo let the jab go. Lop was hungry, so there'd be no getting the last word.

Please hide.

Lop obeyed, if reluctantly.

Ragin knocked at the kitchen door. They received a sour look from the housemistress, but Ragin's silly robes won them entrance. "I'll send a boy to ask if Lady Quinn wants anything to do with you." Her eye lingered on Fallo's single, thick black eyebrow. Something akin to pity crossed her face. "I'll see if I can find a muffin to spare for you lads." She bustled off.

Quinn Peline arrived less than a minute later, wearing riding jacket and jodhpurs. Gauging from the redness in her cheeks she had run the entire way. "You know where Kila Sigh is?"

They hadn't mentioned Kila to the housemistress. Their hesitation in answering was all the answer

Quinn needed. She shooed them into the butler's office and shut the door. "Tell me."

It didn't take long, and when Fallo mentioned that Kila was being held by the Way of Til, Quinn's mouth clamped into a thin line. Her eyes were fury. She drew in a breath, then pulled her dark hair back and cinched it with a leather tie. "I'll ring for the carriage."

"We can't be recognized," Fallo said. "My father wants me dead, and his . . ." Fallo didn't know. He looked to Ragin.

"He wants me to come home, begging for forgiveness. But I won't. Ever."

Quinn opened the office door and start shouting orders. Servants and maids scurried like startled pigeons. In moments Ragin was being pulled out of his robes and stuffed into fine shirt and trousers. Fallo's too-short and too-tight clothes were left on his person, but a cloak fell over his shoulders and then a wiry man of seventy cinched it at the throat with nimble fingers. The wool was light and fine, a tight weave sure to keep the damp off.

As they trundled from the house, the housemistress thrust muffins into their hands. Lop hopped into the carriage just as a footman was starting to close it. The man let out a squawk of surprise, quickly muffled as the door slammed shut. The carriage started to roll before they took their seats.

"Another Beloved One," Lady Quinn said, eyeing

Lop. "Much different from Kila's companion. I had assumed they all looked alike."

Lop presented herself for petting and Quinn obliged. "Now, lads. Tell me your plan."

Fallo looked at Ragin, who looked back at him. Fallo cleared his throat in embarrassment. "You see, with Kila there isn't so much planning as there is just doing stuff willy-nilly."

Quinn arched an eyebrow. "That worked out wonderfully, didn't it?" One hand dropped to a dagger at her belt. The sheath was plain black leather worked with black metal trim. Even the hilt was black. It reminded Fallo of Cayne, Kila and Wen's family blade.

"Here's how we do things," Fallo said, pointing at Lop who had deigned to use Quinn's lap as a bed. "I can speak to Lop. She can speak to the other cats. If Nax and Huff are alive in the Abbey, Lop will be able to find out where they are."

"Useful. But who is Huff?"

"That's Henley's cat."

"Who's Henley?"

Ragin made a choking noise. "Not Henley Mast, surely."

"Why not?"

Ragin blanched, but didn't say more.

Quinn leaned forward and snapped her fingers. "Pay attention, you two. Who is Henley Mast?"

Fallo shrugged. "A friend of mine and Kila's. He

was captured by Donse Masters. And tortured. The same way Kila is being tortured."

"Tortured?" Ragin cried. He was echoed by Quinn. Fallo realized he probably shouldn't have mentioned that part. They didn't need any new worries added to those they already had. But now that he was thinking about it, he realized he didn't know why Quinn was helping them at all.

"Kila never mentioned knowing a Radiant," Fallo said.

"I'm not the Radiant. My mother is. The Voluptuary sent me to fetch Kila and Wen. I don't know how the Voluptuary knew, but she told me where to wait, and sure enough Kila came by, carrying her brother over her shoulders. I invited her to sleep at the house. Then she ran off."

"So you work for the Voluptuary?"

"I do her favors from time to time."

Fallo recalled that Yiqa did the same, as well. He wondered just how many people the old lady had under her thumb. He resolved that when this was all over, he'd stay as far from the Baths as he could.

"So why are you helping us?" he asked.

Quinn's eyes crinkled. "Because I know what Kila is."

Ragin looked as confused as Fallo. "What, exactly, do you think she is?" the boy said.

"She's a Shadline." She drew her dagger and flourished it, sending it tumbling across the top of her hand, then spinning over her thumb. The blade flipped a bit wildly into the air at the end of the trick. She managed to snag it by the hilt before it hit the floor. With a swift practiced motion, she returned the blade to its sheath. "As am I."

Ragin looked at Fallo and they both burst out laughing. Their mirth wasn't long-lived. Quinn's left eyebrow was doing that arched thing that women did. A look that always made Fallo feel young and foolish. Still, she had nearly fumbled the blade during her flourishes. No Shadline would do that.

"I did not say Kila was trained," Quinn said. "But once a Shadline blade chooses a person, they are a Shadline forever. As such, she has duties to the order, and I have duties to her."

The carriage rounded a sharp bend and continued a rapid descent toward the Trialti Arch and Dunne Medow Plaza.

"But this is good," Ragin said. "If you are truly a Shadline—and I don't doubt your word—then you can go in and get Kila out. No Donse Master can stop you."

"I cannot attack every Donse Master who stands in my path. I have taken oaths against just such a thing. We must use stealth mind trickery."

Fallo's mood soured further. Why was it that everyone with any useful ability took oaths not to use it? Suspicion rose, tingling his scalp. He pretended to look out the window, but studied Quinn's reflection in the glass. He had never heard of a Shadline announcing themselves. In fact, the legends all said a Shadline kept her skills secret, lest she be challenged to duels and have to kill a bunch of idiots.

And Quinn sure seemed overeager to sneak into the Abbey. As if such a thing could be done at all.

Nax is gone, Lop sent. *Huff is in the Abbey, but I cannot speak to him.*

It was unusual for Lop to volunteer any information at all, much less accompanied by waves of worry. Fallo remembered the muffin in his hand. He broke off a chunk and offered it to Lop. The cat sniffed it and gobbled it down.

"How should we go in?" Ragin asked. "There are side entrances to the Abbey, but we would get lost instantly once inside."

"We'll go in the front entrance to the Cathedral," Quinn said. "You two will pretend to be my servants."

What do you mean Nax is gone? Fallo sent.

Gone. The way Huff was for a while.

Ragin pulled his cloak more tightly around himself. "And what pretext will you offer to the Donse Master on duty to get us farther inside?"

Quinn considered a moment, then said, "I'll explain that I wish to make a sizable donation, and might I speak with Highest Binel. Meanwhile, you two can skulk off in search of your friends. I'll keep the Donse Master on duty distracted."

Fallo didn't like much of what she'd said, except

that one part about skulking. That made sense. "One problem. Whether we succeed or fail, they'll remember you were involved."

"Leave that to me."

The carriage drew to a stop. They had come to the great front steps of the Cathedral.

Lop, anything from Huff?

No. But I can feel his fear. And anger.

They tumbled from the carriage and walked up the steps. The Cathedral loomed above them, spires disappearing in the murky overcast, gargoyles vomiting rainwater to the stones far below.

24

———

TO HAVE AN ALLY

Decades of experience had honed the Hargothe's skill with pain. Usually the subject's heart failed, but not Kila's. Instead, she had fallen into a dreamless unconsciousness. Ideal, really. It allowed him to expend much less effort exploring the landscape of her mind.

The Beloved One, too, had slipped into a profound sleep. The Hargothe knew where and how their minds were connected. A remarkable weave of infinite complexity.

The Hargothe studied it, probing with mercusine thoughts. One of the acolytes had placed the animal on the bed next to him. He had his hand on the soft, warm body. Such a pleasant sensation.

He did not possess the strength to fully occupy the girl's mind. Not that he wanted to. A female body was born tainted, possessed of all the basest urges and irrationalities of animals. But taking the girl's Beloved One would serve him. For then she would be defenseless, and he could drain her mercusine powers as easily as swallowing a cup of tea.

And what power!

But first, the Beloved One. Yes, it was despised of Til, but that was because it served those who served Kil. When brought into the Hargothe's service, his righteousness would bring the animal's power into the cause of light.

Removing the bond from Kila and placing it into his own mind was a delicate task. He doubted the finest seamstress in Her Enlightened Majesty's wardrobe possessed a tenth the skill he now wielded.

It was helpful to listen to the mercusine, rather than see it. With such a perspective, a knot became a harmony. He merely injected a dissonant note, a clash that made the interwoven spirits recoil.

And there was the opening he needed.

Now, he was back to viewing the mercusine, threading his own thoughts through and snipping off Kila Sigh's.

The bond settled into his mind like a pleasantly heavy blanket. Lovely.

"One of you acolytes, go fetch Highest Binel," he said. His voice was faint even to his own overly-sensitive ears. "And tell my servant to fetch a length of twine. I wish to secure this animal to the bedpost."

"Yes, Seer Hargothe."

He heard the rustle of clothing and the soft gasp of the door opening and closing. To the remaining novitiate he said, "Watch the girl. She will be distraught upon awakening. And put that blade of hers in your belt."

The dagger strike to his throat had been a shock. The ward he'd placed upon his body had never been tested, and now that it was expended he lacked the strength to reform it.

The girl would provide him with plenty of power. He needed only to rest an hour or so. Even to drain a subject required some power. Power he now lacked.

He prodded the cat, wishing it would awaken. He longed to speak to it. It would be nice to have an ally, one who he knew was absolutely loyal. Now he had it. And with the Beloved One's bond, his own strength would multiply. A wonderful benefit indeed.

The cat did not awaken. But it would eventually. And when it did, he would know the location of all the others like it. Lovely.

25

MY EYES AFIRE

Henley and Huff crouched in a patch of dimness between two widely-spaced lanterns. The corridor ahead was currently blocked by a remarkable confrontation.

Two acolytes and a young Donse Master were staring down Dunne Yples, who screamed at them to step aside and unlock the door.

The acolytes stood behind the young Donse Master, a man with a splotchy round face. The Donse Master held his hands up as he offered calming words. Dunne Yples was having none of it. And he was the only one armed.

He lunged, swinging his oak plank. The young Donse Master leaned away, taking the blow on his forearm. A horrific crack resounded down the corridor. Henley winced at the familiar sound of breaking bone. He'd heard such aboard his father's ship during his time there learning the ropes.

Dunne Yples was not done. He set about pounding the young man to the floor until one of the acolytes ducked between them and shoved his shoulder into Yples' gut. The two slammed to the floor, fists and feet blurring.

Henley had seen more skilled fighting in Cheapsgate alleyways. Neither man had the first clue. The second acolyte did not seem much interested in joining the fray. And given how badly Dunne Yples smelled, Henley couldn't fault him.

The young Donse Master was moaning, but he didn't move. Henley decided the moment called for boldness.

Wait here, he sent to Huff. He ran forward, waving his arms and screaming.

The acolyte's face went white. Henley could only imagine how he looked, ginger hair matted with filth, face begrimed, eyes wild. Instead of charging the man, Henley stopped at the next cell and jerked the door bar free. Then the next, and the next.

Yanking cell door after cell door open, he shouted for the prisoners inside to run free. But only smells came out.

Your scheme is failing, Huff sent. *Try knocking the men down.*

Thank you. You're so helpful.

You're welcome.

Henley barely had the strength to carry one of the planks, let alone swing it. Perhaps a bit of Fallo's bravado might work.

Straightening, he shouldered the plank and tried to look menacing. Dunne Yples screamed Dem-Kisk at his opponent's face, spittle flying. His opponent had gotten a momentary advantage, having straddled the madman and pinned his arms to the floor. Blood flowed from Yples' nose.

As Henley got closer, he saw the young Donse Master's head was lying in a pool of blood. He was no longer moaning.

The remaining acolyte was fumbling with the door lock.

"Don't you dare run away," Henley said, hoping the man would do just that. "I mean to beat your head to jelly then eat it with a spoon."

The acolyte—a man in his mid-thirties, with an egg-shaped head too small for his body—screamed and finally unlocked the door. He pushed through and sprinted away.

Henley stopped next to the acolyte still straining to hold Dunne Yples down. Henley decided not to think about it. He swung his plank, taking the man in the back of the skull. He slumped over, suddenly boneless.

Yples shoved him off and sprang to his feet. A gash on his forehead dripped blood into his eyes. Rather than sensibly wipe it away with his sleeve, he blinked furiously and screamed. "Dem-Kisk! The world gone black! My eyes afire!"

Henley prodded him in the belly with his plank. "The Hargothe has the girl. Where is his chamber?"

A moment of lucidity came over the man and he did finally wipe the blood from his eyes. "The Hargothe is down there." He started walking as if there were no urgency at all.

But the acolyte who had just run off would surely be fetching more Donse Masters. Henley remembered the one who had captured him, the one with the rod that made Henley's body freeze up. They had to get Kila and get out before that one showed up.

"Hey, Dunne Yples. What were you saying earlier? Something about Dem-Kisk?"

Like pulling the trigger on a flickbow, Yples shot forward, shrieking his warnings anew. Henley chased after, Huff slinking along the wall far behind.

26

TILSDAY PIOUS

The Donse Master on duty in the Cathedral of Til was a sour-faced man of seventy. His cheeks were clean-shaven, but a whiff of wine came from him every time he spoke. Which was often.

"I 'preciate your generosity, Lady. If you'll entrust your coin to me, I'll see to it that Highest Binel himself writes you a receipt."

Lady Quinn Peline had a particular skill with looking imperious. With her hands on her hips, and chin lifted, she seemed to be looking down at a man at least a hand taller than she.

Fallo made his way to the chapel of Mayla, the daughter of Til, killed in the first moments of her life by the dragon Anaxanthes. The Donse Masters used the chapel for storage. Mayla was not a true goddess in their eyes, so they didn't think she warranted much respect.

The chapel was an ideal place for Fallo to release Lop from under his cloak. Ragin stood guard. "I believe the Lady Peline is not fully in her mind."

"You noticed, eh? Well, at least she's on our side."

Lop scurried into the shadows. Convincing her of the mission's necessity had not been all that difficult. Convincing her to do her part had required outright bribery. If successful, Fallo was going to have to procure an entire roast chicken for the gluttonous beast.

Huff is on the move, Lop sent. *Henley was freed from his cell by a stinky madman. Nax is still gone. And remember, I get the entire bird. Not just a wing and a leg.*

I'll remember. Where are they?

Down. Here. A flash of the catsight came into Fallo's mind. A view from the pulpit looking down at a stairwell surrounded by wrought-iron railing.

Fallo knew it. "This way." He strode across the nave, not caring if a Donse Master spotted him. With Lady Peline arguing—quite loudly—about not accepting a receipt without the Highest offering a personal blessing, all attention was elsewhere.

There were only a few Donse Masters about. Several parishioners were seated in the nave, absorbed in their meditations upon the glory of Til. Or whatever it was the devout did. Fallo's father was "Tilsday pious and Kil-kissing blasphemous for the rest of the ten-day."

Fallo and Ragin kept their hoods up, which was—strictly speaking—not allowed in the Cathedral. Nobody stopped them.

Lop met them at the top of the stairs. A sign warned: TIL'S SERVANTS ONLY. The scuff of hurried footfalls sounded from below. Fallo and Ragin backed behind a column and watched as a frazzled acolyte appeared and dashed away.

Lop slipped down the steps, belly swinging side to side below her. Fallo cursed and followed, Ragin stumbling after.

"Kila will be the death of me," Ragin mumbled.

"That's if you're lucky."

27

HOW IT SCALDED

Kila woke crying.

She wiped her nose on her sleeve and clamped her teeth shut. But still her chest convulsed. No words came to mind. No coherent thought, either.

The spike-pain of the Hargothe's intrusions left a dull ache in her head. Her scream-torn throat burned. Her dry eyes stung, forcing her to squint even in the dim of the Hargothe's crypt.

But bodily discomforts were no more to her than a vague itch. For inside her was nothing at all.

Everything joyful had been extinguished. The sun had gone out. The ocean dried up. The savor of bread turned to ash. The laughter between companions silenced.

Nax!

There was no response. There could be no response. The gentle, warm presence of Nax in her mind had vanished.

With wooden movements, she pushed onto her knees. "Naxie!"

The Hargothe lay on his bed. She did not give him a moment's thought. She had to find Nax. She had saved her once, she could do it again. *Til, Ori, Pol! Please!*

An acolyte embraced her from behind, pinning her arms. She kicked and squirmed. But even as the frenzy of terror erupted, the strength in her limbs seeped away.

Nax lay on the bed next to the Hargothe. The man's hand rested on Nax's head. The slim gray was breathing.

Nax lived. The shock of relief pulled the breath from Kila. She went limp.

Nax. Why did you leave me?

The Hargothe's skull-like head turned toward her. His lips parted, a grimace or smile, Kila couldn't tell. In his face, terror and glee were the same.

That's when she knew. He had done this. He had severed the bond.

He whispered, "Acolyte, there is a commotion in the hall. Please release the girl and see what transpires."

The acolyte let Kila go. Her knees buckled and she

fell. She reached for the mercus. Metal glow flared all around. The lantern, the hinges on the door, nails in the bed frame. The glows intensified with her fury.

The Hargothe spoke into her mind, *I feel the mercusine welling within you. Excellent.*

She jerked her head up, scanning him with her mercus vision. The flow of blood in the Hargothe's body was as faint as a sliver-moon on a cloudy night. But it was there.

She recalled the weird place the demayne had taken her. Where Dunne Marlow had been waiting. The columns with the symbols. She had added to the glow of the symbol, the three slashes. Something had happened there, causing her to be thrown backward.

She bent her thoughts upon adding to the glow of the Hargothe's blood. She would turn him to ash. She would burn every acolyte and Donse Master in the Abbey. And then she would bring the Cathedral down, a tomb of rubble for all of them.

You give me what I am too weak to take, Kila Sigh. Til is great!

Her sense of pushing into the glow shifted, jerking from her control. Now the glow pulled at her. At the same time, her arms stiffened and she bent at the waist. On all fours, she crawled toward the bed—against her will.

She had felt this twice before, most recently when the demayne had used it against her. The Voluptuary had called it willshifting.

Oh, Til is great indeed. For he sent you to strengthen me.

The mercus exploded in sensation. The Hargothe's stale breath, his sweat, his bodily filth made her gag. Somewhere beyond the door a man screamed, "Dem-Kisk!"

The mercus glow of the Hargothe's blood flared. And though she closed her eyes, she saw it still. Nax's, too.

Her hands raised to grip the side of the bed. Muscles contracted to pull her body upright, then bent her to lie next to the sickly old man. Inside she recoiled, but her limbs obeyed his commands.

His body absorbed the warmth from hers. The willshift jerked her arm out to embrace his wasted torso. The Hargothe guided her hand to his wrist, then forced her to pull it toward her face, where his palm finally came to rest on her cheek.

Revulsion had no power to move her. Even the impulse to scream was forbidden to her.

I possess your Beloved One. Now I shall possess your power.

The flow of her mercus grew, adding to the glow of his blood. But it did not burn him. Kila felt the outflow as a gout of fire shooting from her mind to his. The Hargothe forcibly wrenched her very essence from her, as if he reached spidery fingers into her abdomen and yanked out her guts.

Nax!

The cat was just across the Hargothe's narrow torso from her, stretched out, limbs askew. It wasn't the pose of slumber, but of a lifeless creature carelessly tossed. Her flank rose and fell in long breaths. A length of twine was cinched around her neck in a slip-knot. It trailed to a post at the foot of the bed. Kila's anger and terror magnified at the sight. But the Hargothe controlled both her mercus and body. Neither rage nor desperation had the slightest effect.

As her power flowed to the Hargothe, the shouts in the hallway grew louder. "Dem-Kisk! Dem-Kisk!"

The door burst open, sending a waft of breeze across Kila. With her senses so enlivened it felt like an icy gust.

"Seer!" an acolyte said, struggling to keep his voice low. "Bloodshed in the corridor. Prisoners escaped. Dunne Yples and the boy. They have—" Kila could not see him, for the Hargothe had willshifted her eyes to look upon his hideous face. He had drawn her close, so that she nestled against him like a lover.

The acolyte let out a grunt. The sounds of a scuffle roared in her ears. A wooden crack ended it. Heavy breathing and sewer-reek filled the chamber.

"Dem-Kisk! Thinnies into flames!"

"Kila?"

She recognized the second voice. Henley.

"Dunne Yples!" Henley cried. "No!"

Pain exploded in Kila's shoulder, sending red

flashes across her vision. The Hargothe gasped and jerked. Nax startled awake, leapt to her feet, and let out a horrific scream.

28
____

MOLASSES TIME

Henley charged at Dunne Yples' back, but not before the crazy Donse Master had swung his plank at Kila again. The board chunked into Kila's shoulder, this time making a rending noise as the wood split from the force of the impact.

Henley swung his plank at Yples' back. The blow staggered the man, but he didn't turn to fend Henley off. Instead, he raised his board for a third time. "Dem-Kisk!"

Kila didn't so much as raise her arm to protect herself. Henley leapt onto the Donse Master's back, bracing his own plank against the man's throat and pulling back. Together they fell, the weight of the man's thick torso crushing Henley as they impacted the floor.

Henley did not let go. Dunne Yples clawed at the

board, his breath cut off. Gurgling noises spewed from his lips.

Huff blurred past and hopped onto the bed. A horrific mewling rose a moment later.

Huff!

But the cry wasn't coming from Huff.

Huff sent, *It's Nax. She . . .*

Dunne Yples rolled, carrying Henley with him. With strength beyond his size, the man scrabbled to his knees, Henley hanging on to the plank and pulling it into the man's throat. But mere strangulation would not stop Yples.

Gripping his own half-broken plank, the Donse Master spun and lunged at Kila.

Something tore in Henley's mind, a rift that turned the world green, as if the lantern on the wall emitted a mossy light, tinging all it touched.

Incredibly, Dunne Yples' motions slowed. Beyond him on the bed, Huff pawed at Nax, who had pulled back onto her hindquarters, foreclaws up, eyes wide. They all moved like the flow of molasses. The edges of their forms blurred and stretched.

Henley's heart rammed in his chest. Yples' plank was rising again. The butt end had broken, leaving a jagged spike. He was preparing to thrust it into Kila's throat.

The girl lay there, still as death. Her body had snuggled against the Hargothe, his skeletal hand on her face in an almost loving fashion. Her eyes were open, fixed on the corpse-man.

All of this came to Henley in long, slow seconds. Impossibly slow seconds.

Whatever possessed Dunne Yples, he was willing sacrifice breath itself to kill Kila. Henley released his grip on the plank across the man's throat. He dropped to the floor. The cats and the man continued to flow in molasses time.

Henley moved in front of Yples, got his hands on the slowly descending plank and pushed it with all his strength, guiding it away from Kila.

Groaning, sweating, and puffing, Henley shoved the descending spike just far enough that it stabbed into the mattress a bare inch from her neck. It continued to sink, driven by the insane force of Yples' thrust.

Not knowing what else to do, Henley struck the man square in the nose. The flesh compressed, a resounding crunch, low as thunder filled the room. Henley delivered three more in the time the man's head jerked backwards. Yples' arms flailed and he began to totter back on his heels. His eyes rolled up into his skull.

Henley watched him fall. He could have moved to catch the man. He could have taken up a plank and struck him five times before his body impacted the floor. But Henley couldn't move.

Exhaustion like he had never felt—worse even

than after the Hargothe's explorations into his mind—
made his body limp.

The green hue started to fade, then disappeared.
The Donse Master collapsed. Henley joined him on the
floor, tile pressing his cheek. Somewhere behind him,
Nax shrieked as if she had been set on fire.

29

———

LIKE IRON'S GLOW

Why won't you die, Kila Sigh? Why?
The raven flies high above Starside. She hunts for lives.
I feel you, child. You scion of lies.
Why won't you die?

Kila's eyes were open. The waking dream appeared to her as a glowing portal in the wall across the bed, beyond the screaming forms of Nax and Huff. Beyond the agony in her shoulder and arm.

But the view through the window that wasn't there drew her mind the same way the Hargothe drew in her mercusine power. She had no control.

Even her tears could not blur the vision. The raven soared on the winds blown down from the mountains. The Divide lay below her. Starside was quiet beneath the golden hues of sunset. On the other side, Kila's first glimpse of Moonside. But there was nothing to see except the roiling surface of an impenetrable fog, as if storm clouds had descended to engulf the city.

Kila realized the view was from the Citadel. Yes. From the tower itself.

Why won't you die, Kila Sigh?

Why do you lie?

Why?

The Hargothe was screaming, she realized. It wasn't loud, just a shrill whistle coming from deep in his throat. His jaw gaped, and his fetid breath reeked of dead rats and rotten cabbage. Kila discovered she could move.

She pulled away from the old man.

The drain on her mercus had stopped.

Nax?

It took all her strength to press up onto one elbow. Nax was shrieking, eyes wide, fangs flashing. The small animal's gray fur stood straight out. Huff hunched away from her, watching, ready to leap in any direction.

Nax was not looking at Kila, but at the Hargothe. His empty eye sockets were fixed on Nax.

Kila reached for her cat. Nax spat and scratched her hand, then retreated until she was at the edge of the bed.

A moan arose behind Kila.

The Hargothe's body trembled. His chest convulsed. Weak coughs spilled sputum onto his chin.

"Nax? I'm here!" Kila said.

Nax spared her a momentary glance, then renewed her heart-rending mewling. Huff slunk close to Kila, then leapt to the floor behind her.

"Kila?" It was Henley's voice.

Kila twisted to see him, but her shoulder flared in agony at the motion. A glance showed blood staining the shoulder of her shirt.

Henley pulled himself up next to the bed. His face was filthy, eyes red-rimmed and haggard. "Kila, Huff says . . . Huff says the Hargothe took your bond."

He read her look of incomprehension and said again, "The Hargothe took Nax's bond from you."

Sucking air through her teeth, Kila threw her weight on the Hargothe. No amount of pain would stop her. She would wring the life from him.

Her right arm did not respond to her commands except to scream with fiery agony. But her left hand found the Hargothe's throat. He was so emaciated she could get a thumb on one side and the dig her fingers into the other side. Gritting her teeth, she squeezed, expecting to discover the iron hardness that had deflected her blade

Instead, the flesh gave. Her fingernails tore into his papery skin. His jaw dropped wider, his eye sockets squeezed shut. Nax's cries cut off.

Kila was torn away from the Hargothe. Henley was pulling her from the bed.

"Let me—" Kila could not finish her demand, for her injured shoulder jarred as she landed on the floor.

The world went black momentarily, the entirety of Creation becoming a compressed spike of pain as bone shard ground upon bone shard.

Someone was shouting her name. "Kila! Kila!"

Henley lay next to her, his hand patting her cheek. "If you kill him, Nax will die."

Kila realized the zing was upon her, magnifying all her pain. She need only drop it and the agony would diminish. But she would not.

"Help me up."

Henley could barely stand himself. But in slow, unsteady movements, he got to his feet. He spared a glance for the Donse Master on the floor. Blood pulsed from the man's shattered nose.

Kila bit her lip so hard while trying to stand that she tasted blood. Henley spun suddenly. "Lop says Fallo comes!"

Kila barely heard him. She locked her eyes on the Hargothe. The iron in his blood pulsed in her vision. He no longer drained her mercus, for he was in convulsions. Red-tinged spittle bubbled at the corners of his mouth.

He was dying. Not from the superficial damage Kila had caused, but because of something else. Her mind floated over the scene until her eyes landed on Nax. Still spitting and hissing and mewling, the animal fixed her hateful stare upon the Hargothe.

All the feelings Nax had ever passed to Kila now popped to mind. And then Kila knew what was happening. Nax was killing the Hargothe with rushes of hatred, terror, and panic through the bond.

The cat had awoken to discover her bond ripped from Kila and now resting in the Hargothe. The precious, sacred, bond . . . violated.

No wonder Nax rebelled. The horror of the mere notion made Kila's stomach boil with nausea. "Henley, tell Huff to ask Nax to stop sending pain and horror to the Hargothe."

Huff doesn't want to. Huff wants the old man to die.

But didn't you just say that might kill Nax?

Henley didn't answer right away. Then in a burst of frustration he shouted at Huff. "Just tell Nax to stop!"

Abruptly, Nax fell silent. Instantly, the Hargothe's spasms stilled. But his breath remained ragged as he fought for every inhalation.

Kila stumbled close, using her mercus vision to peer into the old man's body. Instinct guided her now, as did desperation. "One of you get that twine off Nax. And see if she'll let you pick her up. I want you to get her out of here."

"I'll do it," Fallo said.

There was mumbling behind her. Henley and another familiar voice. Henley said, "No. Leave her alone."

She closed her eyes, but she could still see the Hargothe's blood. Despite all the mercus he had drawn from her, Nax's assault had wearied him to the brink of death. His heart beat in weak pulses separated by long moments of stillness.

She pressed her ear to the man's chest. Her mercus-enlivened senses brought more information to her mind. She could not have explained it any more than she could explain how to run the roofway. She felt it.

Straightening, she cupped her left hand and swirled, just as she'd seen the demayne do. She put red light, like iron's glow, into her palm. She added heat. The smell of Wen's tincture, freshly brewed, wafted up at her summons. The swirl glowed crimson, and it sang in a high, pure tone.

Gently, she titled her hand, and the mercusine poured like liquid fog onto the Hargothe's lips. He drew it in on a weak inhalation.

His body went rigid, but still the mercusine flowed as if poured from a pitcher rather than Kila's small hand.

And then he relaxed. His chest rose and fell in the deep, easy cycle of a child sound asleep.

"Did you spare some for yourself?" someone said to her. The voice was practically in her ear. Ragin.

She half-turned to him, meeting his awed gaze. He gripped her still-glowing hand, twisted her wrist so that the flow stopped. Then, slowly, he guided it to her own lips.

She breathed in, but the glow of mercusine healing had vanished. Kila collapsed. Ragin barely caught her.

Kila's head fell forward, and only Ragin's arm

around her waist held her upright. Nax was on the floor, being nosed by Huff and Lop.

Fallo helped Henley stay upright. Stumbling like trezz-addled sailors, they left the crypt. In the hall they were stopped by an acolyte and a Donse Master. No. Not a mere Donse Master. He wore vestments of the Highest.

Fallo stepped between him and Kila. "Uncle Binel. It's me, Fallo. Let us pass."

Binel squinted at Fallo. "Til is great! You live. I will personally escort you to your father. Now step aside."

When Fallo refused to move, Binel jerked his head. The acolyte stepped forward and pushed Fallo aside so that Binel could approach Kila. Fallo cursed and struggled, but he was no match for the acolyte.

Highest Binel seemed to forget about his nephew in one second. He studied Kila, drank her in. His eyes held intrigue, fear, calculation. His square jaw and full lips might have made him handsome, but the robes of his office repelled Kila. Cat-killers, all of them.

"Did you do what we asked?" he said.

"No. In fact, I saved his life just now."

"What? Why?"

She did not see the point in explaining. Without knowing exactly what she did, she touched his mind with the mercusine. He fell to the floor. She did the same to his acolyte. Shrugging free of Ragin's grasp she searched the acolyte, retrieving her queller from his pocket.

She slipped it onto her finger, and sighed with relief as the world went numb. Her friends' eyes were upon her. "Get moving!"

They obeyed, Ragin mostly carrying her. They wound up stairs—interminable stairs. Eventually they came into the nave of the cathedral. Fallo led, still supporting Henley, while the cats darted from shadow to shadow.

They kept to the fringes, ducking from side chapel to side chapel. Lop slunk ahead and disappeared.

A moment later, Fallo said, "Lady Peline waits in her carriage outside. It's going to be a tight fit."

"But those Donse Masters at the door will raise the alarm," Kila said. "I can't do to them what I did to Binel. I've got nothing left at all."

"Leave them to me."

Fallo propped Henley against a column then strode to the front entry. There were words. Then three Donse Masters ran toward the rear of the cathedral. Fallo waved for them to come.

Henley managed to move under his own power. Kila's legs gave out before she made it to the door. Ragin scooped her up. The air outside was cold, but fresh. Kila never wanted to smell incense again for as long as she lived.

The cats were already inside the carriage. Soon Kila was lying on the rear-facing bench. The others squeezed in, the vehicle moving before Fallo could swing the door shut.

Warm palms pressed Kila's cheeks. "You left without saying goodbye," Quinn said.

Kila started to apologize, but Quinn winked at her. "Let's get you all to the Baths. Truly. You all need baths."

The carriage wheels clattered over cobblestone as the draft-atlens sped them uphill through Gristenside. Behind them, the great cathedral bell began to toll.

A warm weight pressed on Kila's lap. Nax. The small gray's body trembled. Kila hugged the animal to her.

But there was no connection, no bond. Kila's mind —her very heart—felt as if a great chunk had been torn out.

Tears blurred the world.

30

A MERCUSINE HEALING

Wind ripples across the graygrass fields. The harvest to come will be bountiful. Tenn does not care for harvests or the festival that attends the end of it.

He sits on the wide windowsill in the parlor of the overseer's house. His eyes are closed, his mind submerged in the subtle world of the mercusine. He is not the Hargothe yet. He has not yet heard that word.

Marlow is tottering about the room, under the watchful gaze of Nanny. Little brother is a spark upon the mercusine web, the power that permeates all things and times.

Tenn touches the toddler's mind. A soft probe.

Marlow shrieks and falls onto the rug, cheeks instantly red and damp with tears. Nanny scoops him up. "You silly chicken. Nothing happened at all!"

Tenn wishes his brother no ill will. Nor any particular good. But it is good that he can produce fear in others. He has seen his father the overseer do the same —with threats of physical violence—to good effect on the farm.

Others' minds were weak and vulnerable. Tenn would make his a fortress, one to rival the Citadel in Starside. This thought brought a small smile to the corners of his mouth.

"It is too bright in here," he announced. With careful steps he made his way to the cellar, his favorite place to hide away from the world's constant assault on his senses. Mother tolerated him having a cot there. None knew he slept there every night.

He eased down and folded his hands upon his chest. The mercusine welcomed him into its depths.

"Seer Hargothe!"

He was pulled to wakefulness by a sharp pat on his cheek. A rush of memory filled his mind. The Hargothe sat up.

"Seer!" The elderly servant stepped back. The flutter of his robes and the gasp in the back of his throat betrayed his shock.

And shocked he should be. The Hargothe swung his legs over the side of his bed and stood. The bottoms of his feet felt every flaw in the tile of his crypt. The coppery smell of blood filled the air.

"Who is bleeding?"

"Seer. I do not know. There is blood upon the floor, but no one is here. An acolyte woke me. He said there was—"

"The girl? Where is she?"

"Gone, Seer! As are the boy and Dunne Yples. There are two cell door-bars here. What under Til's great sky has happened? An acolyte found Highest Binel unconscious in the corridor along with acolyte Swilte."

The servant's voice was much too loud for the Hargothe. He lay calm upon the man's mind to quiet him.

The Hargothe straightened, taking a great, slow inhalation. His spine popped and cracked. His ribs expanded, stretching tissue knotted from lying prone so long. He stretched his arms out, flexed his hands, and made fists, delighting in the pops in his knuckles.

He took a step, the first unaided in many years. Then another. He had drained many boys of the mercusine in his decades as the Hargothe, but never had an inflow of their power strengthened him so much. He felt . . . strong.

"I require slippers. Immediately." His voice did not come out a papery rasp, but resonated in the chamber with the force of an orator. He cringed slightly at the volume of it.

"Step into mine, Hargothe! We are of a size, I believe."

Hands took hold of the Hargothe's ankles, guiding his feet into warm slippers.

"Fetch a basin. I mean to wash. And I want proper robes. Hurry, man!"

While he waited, the Hargothe allowed a memory of events to stream in his consciousness. Instantly, he discovered the bond he had stolen from the girl. The Beloved One was still his. But where was it? He scented the air. It had been here, but was no longer. Surely the girl had taken the animal when she'd escaped.

But she had done something to him before going. Yes. He remembered now. The animal had attacked him through the bond. Such fury and fright, and no way to stop it. All had faded into blackness, but then the girl had poured warmth into him. A mercusine healing. Kila Sigh had not only saved his life, but she had restored his strength. Miraculous!

The memory was as thin and full of holes as lace. If she had such power, why had she not killed him with it? Why that silly blade attack?

Highest Binel. He had pulled the name from her mind. The man had provided the weapon, hoping she would kill him. Such schemes and intrigues! Marlow had been there, too. He had been part of the betrayal. No surprise.

The elderly servant returned. He guided the Hargothe to a basin of steaming water. "Let me help you out of your gown, Seer."

"Leave me. I will attend to myself. You will know when I want your assistance."

"But, Seer—"

"Go!"

31

SO MUCH TAKEN

The Voluptuary and three Sensuals met the carriage outside the Baths of Ori. Kila's legs wobbled as she stepped from the carriage. A man she did not know took her by the elbow, then caught her up in his arms as she sagged.

"Get her inside," the Voluptuary said. "By Ori's grace! What is this?"

"This is Henley," Fallo said. "I know he looks like a swirehog, but he's actually quite well-mannered once you get to know him."

"Your animals may enter," the Voluptuary said. "And Lady Peline, I would have a word with you. There are several things . . ."

Kila didn't hear the rest. Sens Beth of the Great Bosom had taken charge of her, leading the man carrying her into the Baths and straight to a cot. Finta Sahng was busily stirring a concoction at a side table.

The ancient woman didn't even turn. "My sister tells me she felt a great welling of the mercusine. I suppose that was you exhausting yourself again."

Kila pressed her filthy palms to her face. "Nax? Where are you?"

"The gray one?" Sens Beth said. "She's hiding under the reception desk."

The boys straggled in. The stench clinging to Henley wafted to Kila's nose. A hand pressed her shoulder. She lowered one hand from her face and opened an eye. Ragin was leaning over her.

"Fallo told me about Nax. I'm sorry. But after what you did . . . Isn't there some way to get her back? If the Hargothe could do it to you, why can't you—"

"I don't know how! I don't know how!"

"And you never will if you do not train." The Voluptuary's voice was firm but not angry. "Ragin, return to your room. We'll discuss your penance for leaving without permission later."

Ragin knelt and brushed Kila's brow with his warm hand. "I wish I could help you. I want you to know that I will do anything . . ."

"Raginalt!" the Voluptuary barked.

The boy straightened. Kila caught his hand, tears again blurring her vision. He seemed made of light in that moment, with a brazier behind him and his shock of blond hair aglow.

"Let him go, child," Sens Beth said.

Kila released Ragin's hand and he slipped away.

The Voluptuary took his place next to her. The man who had carried Kila in brought the woman a chair.

Kila was vaguely aware that Fallo and Henley had gone. As if reading her mind, the Voluptuary said, "They will stay here for a night. Perhaps two. I will see them fed and bathed. Bathed first, I think."

"They are both in danger if recognized." Kila wiped her eyes. "That is Fallo PiTorro and Henley Mast."

"I know who they are."

"Then you know they are in danger if discovered."

The woman turned and motioned. Yiqa appeared and bent close. The Voluptuary whispered some instructions and the Alnassi woman flowed away like a shadow retreating from light.

"He took Nax," Kila said, trying to keep the tremble from her voice. "He *took* her. She's not"—Kila pressed her chest, eyes burning—"not here."

Suddenly the Voluptuary's arms were around Kila, her warmth pressing against Kila's cheek. Sens Beth made more soft crooning noises.

Finta brought a stool to the other side of Kila's cot and took Kila's hands. The old woman met the Voluptuary's gaze. Both looked stricken.

Something else was wrong. Kila sensed it the way she sensed the mercusine. "What is it? What aren't you telling me?"

The Voluptuary squeezed Kila tighter. A warm tear fell from her cheek and onto Kila's forehead. "It's your brother. Ori drew him into the depths not a quarter of an hour ago."

"No. No. Nax would have . . ." But Nax couldn't have.

Finta put a warm tea cup in Kila's hands. The Voluptuary propped her up. "Drink. It will help you sleep. And forget, for a while."

"Wen isn't dead. He wouldn't leave me."

"Drink."

Kila obeyed, cup shaking such that half the tea spilled in her lap. Warmth spread through her limbs; her body slumped against the Voluptuary.

Wen wouldn't leave her. Without him, who would tell her not to talk Cheaps so much? Who would smile when she brought home a purse full of gold skillets? Who would remind her of Father's dream to set up as legitimate recovery agents? Who would be proud of her?

"The poor dear," Finta said. "So much taken from her all at once."

The Voluptuary heaved a great sigh. "It is well that she sleeps. For she will soon be asked to give more. Much more."

"Can she ever find peace?" Sens Beth asked.

"I doubt she will go looking for peace. Not now. Pray she does not shatter the world for vengeance."

32

UNBLOCK YOURSELF

"I haven't seen these quarters since I was raised to the robes," Dunne Marlow said. He sat in a gilded chair across from Highest Binel. The head of the Way of Til in Starside looked wan, and his hand trembled as he lifted his goblet to his lips.

"Who was Highest then?" Binel asked. He darted a glance to the door again, the tenth time at least since the two men had come to sit in the Highest's private quarters. Whatever that girl had done to him, he was well and fairly spooked by it. He had no interest in Marlow's small talk, but seemed reluctant to get to the important topic. Namely, Kila Sigh and what had happened—or not happened—to the Hargothe.

"Nare Simyn," Marlow said, grinning in remembrance. "He was one hundred and fifty years old. Spry as a teenager, if a bit deaf."

"You don't say." Highest Binel produced a kerchief

from a robe sleeve and patted his forehead. The chamber was not warm, despite the fire and lush rugs and tapestries. A window was open, admitting a chill wind, edged with winter.

So the man was not going to dive into the story, Marlow thought. Might as well pull it from him. "My brother still lives and Kila Sigh has escaped."

Highest Binel's lips went white. He set his goblet on a side table and pinched the bridge of his nose. "Did anyone tell you about Dunne Yples."

"My little mice have squeaked a rumor or two. Went mad in the thinnie's cavern town, no?"

"That girl ashed a hundred of them. Yples witnessed it. He's been screaming Dem-Kisk ever since."

"Yes. I'm aware. Why are we talking about Yples? I thought you had him locked in a cell."

"Escaped. Along with a boy the Hargothe was using. That boy, along with two interlopers, rescued the girl right from the Hargothe's crypt."

"Escaped? Someone here let them out?"

"No. Yes. I know not. But Yples is gone."

"Did he go with the girl?"

Highest Binel didn't answer. He lifted his eyes, slowly, until he finally met Marlow's gaze. "What if he's not as mad as he seems? I faced the girl. She dropped me and a novitiate as if we were bits of refuse." He snapped his fingers. "Such power has not been known for an age. I thought the old texts that spoke of such were exaggerations. Legends."

"Why didn't she kill him?" Marlow asked, a growing unease making sweat prickle along his spine. "Did you provide the blade?"

"I did. The acolyte attending her said the blade glanced from the Hargothe's throat as if from armor."

Of course it had. Marlow had developed that technique, but he hadn't shared it with his brother. Apparently the wily old man had figured it out on his own. It would have taken an enormous reserve of mercus strength, probably formed over months of concentrated effort. Even now, Marlow's defense against physical attack was only a fraction of what it had been.

He laughed. The girl had tried to stab him and the Hargothe on the same day and had been foiled by the same technique. Only Pol knew the chances of that. His mirth died as quickly as it had risen.

"What if she is Dem-Kisk?" Highest Binel said. "We are wholly unprepared. And given the treatment she's endured, there is little guarantee she will fall on the side of Right when it comes to it."

The outer door opened. Highest Binel turned, anger furrowing his brow. He had told the guard on duty that no one was to interrupt them.

The man's anger turned to fear when the Hargothe stepped in, dressed in Donse Master robes and walking under his own power. His wispy white hair was slicked back on his skull.

Marlow stood, eyes scanning the room for a way out. The window stood open. How far was the drop? Thirty feet? His hand went to his collar, felt the queller under his robes. His brother would not be able to touch his mind.

Highest Binel had no such protection. "Seer Hargothe," he said, voice shaking. "It is good to see you so well."

"I pulled your traitorous words from that girl's mind, Binel." Two guards entered, silver breastplate polished to mirror shine, cloaks of scarlet draping to the floor. Their swords were drawn. Surely, the Hargothe had touched their minds. Perhaps they were not being willshifted, but a strong impulse had made them obedient to the Hargothe's commands, even though he had no authority over them.

Marlow edged away from Binel and toward the window. That truly was his only way out of this alive. If the Hargothe knew Binel's involvement . . .

"Plant your feet, Marlow," the Hargothe said, turning his eyeless gaze on him. His voice was strong. Stronger than in his youth. "I know of your treachery."

Binel suddenly went up on tiptoes, his arms rigid at his sides. Eyes wide, his breath shook, and his whole body trembled.

The Hargothe walked around him, then stopped to

face him. Marlow had seen his brother do this trick many times as youths, when Tenn had taken to blotting out his vision with a black scarf fastened over his eyes. This was true willshifting, and it chilled Marlow to the marrow to see.

"I raised you to this position, Binel. You thank me with duplicity."

Binel tried to answer, but only choking sounds came out of his mouth. And then a trickle of blood. He had bitten his tongue.

Quelled as he was, Marlow could not sense the mercus tricks the Hargothe used. But he had not suspected his brother so strong. He must have gained much from draining the girl.

Marlow was surprised to discover his own dismay. Not only at his brother's newfound strength, but also at the unhappy fate of Kila Sigh.

But she had retained some power. Enough to drop Highest Binel. She still lived. Dem-Kisk or not, she still lived.

Marlow made his decision. In five long strides, he made it to the window. He peered out. It was a long drop. He would certainly break both of his legs. But there were vines. Perhaps he could climb down.

The guards stomped after him. Neither said a word, and their eyes were fixed. Marlow swung a leg over the sill, then the other, hands gripping vines. The foliage pulled away. It would never support his weight.

It was jump or surrender. Closing his eyes, he thrust his weight into empty air. He did not fall.

The guards pulled him back through the window and tossed him onto the floor. He looked up to find the Hargothe's robe hem at eye-level. Tenn had always been tall, lanky. But from here, he looked a giant.

"Stand, Brother," the Hargothe commanded. Marlow noticed Highest Binel sitting in the gilded chair, dabbing his lips and nose with a white kerchief, now stained red.

Marlow found his strength and climbed to his feet, though his legs trembled with the nervous excitement of one who had thrown himself to probable death and survived.

The Hargothe's eye sockets were red, but Marlow felt the eerie certainty his brother was looking at him, impossible as that was.

"Her Enlightened Majesty has agreed to have you at the Citadel. I met my side of the bargain. And I know from sifting Kila Sigh's thoughts that you met your side by retrieving her for me. This misunderstanding about having me murdered is a complication."

A complication. The Hargothe was toying with him as he had done throughout their childhood, always thinking up tortures that left no mark upon Marlow's skin for Father and Mother to see.

"I was trying to save you the trouble of killing me,

by doing it myself just now," Marlow said, finding his voice much steadier than he expected.

"But I don't want you dead. You have valuable skills. I intend to use them."

The demayne. The very thing that had gotten him expelled from the Way of Til was going to save his neck. The irony was delicious.

"What do you need me to do?"

"First, unblock yourself to the mercusine."

The guards took position directly behind him, swords still drawn. Binel was not looking at him. Marlow thought it curious that the Hargothe had let him live, too. But then, having the Highest completely under his sway would be more pragmatic than going through the tedious process of replacing him.

"If I refuse?"

Two stings of pain sprang to life on Marlow's back as the guards pressed the tips of their swords against his flesh.

Marlow lifted his hands to his throat. "It is not a skill I manage unaided. It requires this heller." He pulled the amulet from the throat of his robes and showed his brother the inexpertly carved object.

The Hargothe raised an eyebrow, as if he could actually see it. "A heller?"

"It magnifies mercusine feats of a general nature. I use it to maintain the blocking technique." All lies. A desperate gambit. The amulet itself was a queller.

"Remove it." The Hargothe held out a spindly hand, knuckles swollen, fingers bent.

Marlow obeyed. As soon as he lifted it over his head, the mercus flooded his awareness. Thankfully his brother had bathed recently. The stink of Binel's blood was especially strong in the air.

The Hargothe took the relic, felt the carving with his twisted fingers. Then, just as Marlow expected, he placed the queller over his own neck.

Marlow lunged, knocking his brother back. The guards grunted in surprised as the Hargothe's mercusine power over them vanished. Marlow ran for the outer door. The corridor outside was empty and quiet.

He sprinted—harder than he had ever sprinted before.

The guards' shouts trailed him, but he did not slow. With a flash of mercusine, he set the hall carpets afire behind him.

By the time he stumbled from the abbey, a general alarm had risen. All Donse Masters and acolytes were called upon to douse the flames, leaving no one to chase him.

He slowed to a fast walk, his breath laboring in his chest. He was not used to running. No one pursued him.

I wiilll fiiind you, Marlow, the Hargothe shrieked into his mind. *I willl have vengeance!*

Without his queller, Marlow would never escape

his brother, who had marked him when they were still quite young. Except there was one place . . .

Head down, Marlow stumbled through the night toward the jeweler's shop.

A half hour later, he plunged through the stone wall in the cellar and into what he hoped was a realm out of reach of his brother's senses.

33

SUCH A PRICE

"Lop says Nax went back to him," Fallo said. "I'm sorry."

Kila sat atop a crumbling building in the Blasted Quarter on the outer fringes of Starside. The sun was descending behind the Honor Mountains, sparking golden flares from the spires of the Citadel. The lower quarters stretched below to Kila's left, Gristenside and the cliffs that backed the city to her right. In the hazy distance, the Divide raced in unnatural perfection out to the sea.

Kila had come here to think, despite the real danger of a building collapsing under her. She would welcome it, in fact.

Fallo and Lop sat next to her. The fat cat's eyes squinted against the sun. Henley sat on Kila's left, legs dangling over the edge. Huff was wandering somewhere behind them, hunting chickenbugs.

"Why would Nax do that?" Kila said, not really asking, but thinking aloud. The gaping wound of Nax's absence was still raw, but sleep and food had helped her finally get out of bed and face the day. Her arm was snugged to her belly by a sling Finta Sahng had forced her wear. The pain in her shoulder was nothing compared to that in her heart.

"Lop says she must," Fallo said quietly. "He pulls at her."

Of course he pulled at her. The Hargothe was greedy. He wanted everything Kila had. And she'd felt his strength, his absolute mastery of her mind. How could Nax stand against that?

"I shouldn't have healed him," she said. "Oly is proof of that." Wen was dead, but Oly still lived. The thought that she could have used her mercus healing to cure Wen kept rising to mind. And each time it did, the ache behind her eyes returned.

She kept repeating her father's advice. "If a thought is stabbing you, stop stepping on it."

If only she could put all thoughts out of her mind.

Fallo sneered and looked at his hands. He'd been terribly kind to her, but she knew he didn't like talking about what he called "feely stuff."

He said, "Lop says it's different with Nax and the Hargothe. He did something to the bond. It isn't attached right. Lop can't explain how it's different, but she can feel the danger of it through her connection to

Nax. She is certain that if the Hargothe dies, Nax will die."

Henley coughed into his hand. "Do you think that the reverse is true?"

"We're not killing Nax," Kila snapped. Fallo leaned behind her and punched Henley's arm.

Henley rubbed it. "I wasn't suggesting that."

"Then what were you suggesting?" Kila said.

Henley didn't answer right away. He just looked at her, that new hollowness in his eyes pulling more of the ache to hers. Even with the filth washed from his skin and new clothes on, he held himself like an escaped prisoner expecting to be caught at any moment. His red hair fairly flamed in the sunset, but his eyes absorbed the light.

"I suppose I *was* suggesting that," he said. "I'm sorry. I don't want to hurt Nax. It's just . . . For what that old man did to me. To us. He deserves to die. In agony."

Kila agreed with that last part.

"I'm sorry, Kila," he said.

Kila gave him a smile she didn't have. It took all her will to do it. "I had hoped to free you," she said. "And in the end, you saved me. How can I be mad at you?"

Henley smiled at her, and she was sure it was also an effort for him to do it. He hadn't spoken of his imprisonment. And somehow that made the hurt in him all the more obvious. He'd endured something nobody should have to endure. In that, they were alike.

"It doesn't matter who freed who," Fallo said. "We wanted Henley out and he's out."

"As true as that?" Kila said.

"As true as that," both boys echoed. They watched the sunset in silence.

Fallo scratched his chin, the barely-there wisps of whiskers on it making him look particularly sinister. But there was pain in his eyes, too.

"What is it?" Kila asked, sensing his hesitation.

"I guess this is as good a time as any." He removed a canvas roll from the inside pocket of his jacket and handed it to Kila. "Wen wanted you to have this."

"Father's lockpicks." Kila squeezed the battered roll, letting her fingers drift over the thick strap that cinched it tight.

"He said there was a note inside. He said it was . . . I don't know."

Kila unfastened the strap and unrolled the toolkit. Finely crafted steel probes and hooks were nestled in individual pockets. One had a small round mirror on it, the shaft a series of nesting tubes allowing it to be extended.

"I don't see a note here." Kila was very familiar with the toolkit. There were no pockets for paper.

Fallo shrugged. "Wen wasn't wholly in his mind when he told me to give it to you. He knew what was coming."

"The cost was too high," Henley said quietly. "Why does life demand such a price from us?"

An age-old question. Wen might still be alive if he hadn't taken Huff into the Cathedral. And yet, Kila couldn't fault him for that. And she couldn't blame Henley. Or Fallo.

Life didn't tell you what the price would be. It just claimed it.

The ache in her eyes faded as a different feeling filled her chest. She had trained all her life to recover what was stolen. Wen was beyond the veil of this world. But Nax wasn't.

She tied up the lockpicking tools and tucked the roll into a pocket. "You boys said you were saving money to buy passage on a ship. How much coin do I need to go along?"

Fallo's single eyebrow dipped. "Truly? You wish to go with us? What about Nax?"

Kila breathed in the cold wind, now sharp with winter. "Oh, I'll get her back. Believe me, I will. Then I'm going as far from Starside as the waves will carry me."

34

THROUGH THE BOND

By the time they returned to the Baths, the bell was striking midnight. Sens Beth was on desk duty. She greeted them with a raised eyebrow and disapproving twist of her lips. They had not asked permission to leave.

"I'm glad you're here," she said. "This monster has been raising a ruckus. Raginalt deposited him here so the rest of the novitiates could get some sleep. I've been half-tempted to dunk him in one of the pools."

Oly crept from under her desk, creamy fur spotless. He moved in a way that Kila could only think of as stomping. He nosed Lop and Huff, then jumped onto the Sensual's desk. She squawked and tried to shoo him away.

"Oly, you're being a pest!" Kila said. She moved to pick him up, but he heeled back and spat at her.

Don't touch me!

Then get off the desk. Yer leavin' fur all over Sens Beth's papers. Yer such a—

Kila's knees hit the tiles. A wave of nausea passed through her, then fled, leaving her dizzy. Fallo and Henley knelt on either side of her, faces wrought with worry.

"Get back," she said. "I'm not sobbing. It's just—"

Get out of my head, she sent to Oly.

The cat jumped down and sat just out of reach.

She glared at him. *I don't want you in my head. Get out.*

The bond settled on her, heavy and all wrong. The presence in her mind was nothing like Nax's. It didn't fit, like a shirt too tight under the arms.

Kila stood and screamed at Oly, "GET OUT!"

The cat stood, turned tail, and trotted away. In her mind, his voice came firm and spiteful. *No.*

It took her a long time to sleep. Oly's annoying presence made her sweaty and chilled at the same time. Finally, she got up and asked Sens Beth to take her to the hot pool outside.

As Kila floated beneath the stars, muscles succumbing to the warmth, Oly released the anxiety he had intentionally been sending to her.

I want Nax back, she sent to him.

The answer was long in coming. *So do I.*

Can't we work together?

Oly didn't answer. Summoning the last of her will,

Kila sent warmth and her love for Wen through the bond to Oly.

In answer, Oly went still, the bond seeming to loosen. But he did not release it.

Long after Kila had stepped from the pool, dried herself, and returned to her cot, Oly spoke a final thought into her mind.

Together.

The End of *Mind of Mercusine*
Book Three of Starside Saga

Sign up for "Eric's Elite" to get the **free** Starside short story, *Caverns of Misen-Tine*, an exclusive gift to newsletter subscribers and available nowhere else. *Caverns* is the amazing "origin story" of Fallo. Download it right now at http://bookhip.com/JNPMWX (Pssst! A second Starside Tale, also exclusive, will hit your inbox a bit later.)

More Starside Saga coming!

Kila Sigh's adventures continue in The Raven Throne!

Did you know about the other Starside Tales?

These short stories will take you deeper into the world of Starside. In "Vale of Semūin", a mountaineer named Wenton Sigh stumbles meets an immortal water spirit. In a tale that swims through time itself, discover how Wenton Sigh's momentous decision changed the course of destiny.

In "Name of the Blade" you'll discover how Radiant's daughter, Quinn Peline, came to own her Shadline blade.

Starkiller (Book 3)

Visit ericedstrom.com for a complete list of Eric's fantastic fiction.

Mind of Mercusine